Hard Trail to Breakneck Pass

Bolt is the general foreman for Tug Mackintosh's railroad line, which is competing with Sirus Proctor's railroad to reach Breakneck Pass. Along with a man he befriends in a gunfight, Bolt is charged with the simple task of meeting and bringing Mack's young bride-to-be to the end of tracks.

Arriving just in time to fend off would-be kidnappers, Bolt is smitten by the enchanting Ariette Ekhard. However, within hours of her safe delivery, Ariette is again in the hands of the kidnappers. Bolt mounts a rescue mission, but this time he and his friends are up against overwhelming odds. Trapped and left afoot with the young, society-bred lady, there's little hope of an escape. But Bolt has found something worth fighting for. Against such long odds, she may also be worth dying for.

Hard Trail to Breakneck Pass

Terrell L. Bowers

A Black Horse Western

ROBERT HALE · LONDON

© Terrell L. Bowers 2015
First published in Great Britain 2015

ISBN 978-0-7198-1806-6

Robert Hale Limited
Clerkenwell House
Clerkenwell Green
London EC1R 0HT

www.halebooks.com

Typeset by
Derek Doyle & Associates, Shaw Heath
Printed and bound in Great Britain by
CPI Antony Rowe, Chippenham and Eastbourne

CHAPTER ONE

The Voight family, Mortimer and his three sons, ran roughshod over the residents of the small settlement of Lost Bend, Wyoming. R.L. Bolterfeld – who simply went by the name of Bolt, was the general foreman for the Mackintosh/Ekhard Railroad. He had chosen to spend a few days in town while a new section of railroad was surveyed. Being a visitor, he had no stake in the daily business of the little burg. Even so, he had never had much patience for bullies, and the Voight bunch were a family of bullies.

Like so many settlements throughout the West, smaller communities had no actual lawmen. A few had a county sheriff or city marshal, but many territories had ungoverned counties that were bigger than some states. Often, a judicial-minded citizen would take on the chore of Justice of the Peace, so he could perform or record deaths, marriages and births, oversee contracts and act as magistrate for minor offenses or complaints. But with limited funds and authority, and no actual lawmen available, few of them handled any major court proceedings. When they also lacked the will and manpower to form a vigilante group, it left them near helpless against a vicious band of ruffians.

Bolt was sitting near the window of the tavern, having just finished a bowl of chili and a quarter loaf of bread and honey for lunch, when he saw a stranger ride into town. Mature in looks, the gent appeared to be in his thirties, with thick, albeit neatly shorn, ash-colored hair, a mustache and bushy eyebrows. Average in height, he wore a dusty black suit and a weathered, flat-crowned hat. The man had obviously done a lot of traveling. His horse had alkali dust caked to his hide and stood at the hitch rail with his head hung almost to his knees.

The rider swung stiffly down to the ground, tied off his steed and entered the tavern. He took but a couple steps inside before he paused to sweep his gaze over the patrons.

'Anyone know where I can find Sam Voight?' he asked.

'Seen him and his two brothers a few minutes back,' a man from a nearby table answered. 'The three of them headed for the saloon.'

'Much obliged,' the stranger said. 'How many in the Voight family?'

'Quite a few. The nearest bunch, living outside of town, has the old man and his three boys,' the cordial customer replied. 'Sam had a wife, but she died a short time ago.'

The expression on the stranger's face darkened. 'Yes, I heard about it.' He peered at the other patrons and his gaze came to rest on Bolt. 'Any law hereabouts?'

The same customer was the one to speak up. 'US marshal comes through once or twice a year. That's about it.'

Bolt wondered at being the target of the newcomer's speculative stare and decided he might have thought Bolt was a lawman. He did carry a Colt Peacemaker and had a natural look of authority. Plus, working for the railroad, he was usually attired in the kind of clothes that were somewhat more fashionable than those of most travelers.

The stranger thanked the man who had been amiable, spun on his heel and went out to his horse. Bolt put a coin on the table to pay for his meal and followed him. When he saw the inquisitive man remove a twin-barrel shotgun from the riding boot, he experienced a cold chill. With a glance at the old Navy Colt in the man's holster, he shook his head.

'You did hear the guy inside – there are *three* of them?'

The gent turned a grim expression on Bolt. 'I'll make sure I get Sam before they get me.'

'His wife, the one who died' – Bolt guessed – 'she a relative?'

'My baby sister,' the gent said solemnly. 'Raised her from the time our ma died. She was only seven at the time.'

'Just you and her?'

7

'I was eighteen,' he replied. 'Dad never came back from the war and my younger brother died of fever. When Nancy turned twenty she went to work at a local hospital – wanted to become a doctor one day.' The fellow smiled at the memory. 'She was always bringing home an injured animal or some-thing. We spent two months saving a bird with a broken wing one time. And when I cut my wrist while putting up a fence, she bandaged me up until I could hardly move my arm.'

'Then Sam Voight came along?' Bolt guessed.

'A coupla years back,' the man replied. 'I didn't like him one little bit, but Nancy had stars in her eyes and couldn't see the devil inside of him. The guy arrived with some drovers and met her when he got patched up after a bar fight. A couple weeks later, he married Nancy and brought her from Denver to his family ranch, here in Wyoming.'

His expression became grim. 'I never saw her again. She wrote a few times, but she didn't mention Sam's abuse and drinking problem. It wasn't until she was treated for her injuries by a local medico that I got word Sam was beating her.'

The man lowered his gaze and sadly shook his head. 'I was in the middle of building a shop for a baker and couldn't leave right away. That delay cost my little sister her life.'

'Sam beat her to death?'

'Story given: she fell against the stove and hit her head – accidental death is what he claimed.'

'Could have been an accident,' Bolt cautioned.

'Did you talk to the doctor?'

'He's the one who notified me the first time. I contacted him and he admitted there was some new bruising about her face and ribs ... evidence she had been hit several times before her *accident.*'

'Let's get the law involved,' Bolt said. 'A man who kills his wife deserves to go to prison!'

'Not Voight. And not in Wyoming Territory. They don't have a law on the books about raising your hand agin' your wife or kids. It's a man's right to use a little force to keep his family in line. It would be ruled an accident.'

'These Voights are a brutal bunch,' Bolt cautioned him. 'One of them got into a fight with a gambler some time back. Started out one on one, but the two brothers joined in and they literally beat the guy to death.' Bolt gave a solemn shake of his head. 'The gambler wasn't the one who was cheating, but he's the one who paid the price.'

'You seem a Christian sort and I appreciate the warning,' the determined man said. 'If there was law and justice out here – a certainty Sam would spend twenty years behind bars – I'd go that route. I'm not eager to die, and facing three men, I don't expect to survive. But Nancy was like my own baby girl. I didn't get here in time to save her, but I'm going to make certain that animal never hurts another woman.'

Bolt removed the leather thong from the hammer of his gun, lifted it in his holster and let it slip back into place. He didn't want to get involved in another man's fight, but right was right. A savage husband had battered, brutalized, and finally killed his wife. No man should get away with that.

'Maybe I'll tag along with you,' he offered. 'If I can keep Sam's brothers out of the fight, you might live to see another day.'

'I can't ask you to do that!' the man protested. 'Damn, young fella, I'd feel like ten kinds of a sinner if I got you killed.' He stared incredulously at Bolt. 'Besides which, I don't even know your name.'

'It's Bolterfeld, but I go by Bolt,' he introduced himself. 'And there has to be justice in this part of the country, even when there isn't a lawman around.'

'I'm Deacon Johnston – my friends call me Deek.'

'Reckon that acquaints us,' Bolt stated. He stuck out his hand. 'Proud to meet you, Deek.'

'Likewise,' Deek responded, taking his hand in a firm shake.

'Now that we're practically lifelong pals, let's see about collecting for your sister.'

Deek did not hide his fascination. 'I can't believe you're ready to do this. I mean, you never met me before and didn't even know my sister.'

'No, but I have two sisters of my own. If any man ever raised a hand to one of them, and I wasn't available, I would appreciate having someone of good conscience set the abuser straight.'

Deek checked the loads in his scatter-gun and the two of them started off in the direction of the saloon. No more chatter, no plan of action, just two men intent upon seeing justice done!

Ariette Ekhard stormed about her father's office, waving her arms and ranting with ire. Her oaths bordered on, but never quite breached disrespect as she wailed her extreme displeasure at the top of her lungs. She had never been so angry, so hurt, or felt so utterly estranged in all of her life.

Brock Ekhard remained immobile, sitting in his leather-bound chair with both hands firmly clasped on the desktop. He had made up his mind and that would be the end of it. However, his iron will did not crush Ariette's own spirit. She finally stopped circling the room and came to stand opposite him, hands on her hips, fire glowing in her eyes.

'What kind of father sells his own daughter into a life of humiliation and servitude?' she challenged. 'How can you make me into a personal slave for some dirty-minded, overstuffed, ancient, railroad tycoon?'

'Mr Mackintosh is a businessman and a gentleman.' Her father defended the man. 'He will treat you like a queen.'

'But . . .' she sputtered, 'but how can you expect me to marry a man I've never even met?'

Brock's face worked, but he remained calm, in control of his emotions, as always. 'Ariette, my dear, I implore you to look at this from the logical standpoint. Every cent we have is tied up in that railroad. Our family fortune stands to be lost if we don't make this joint arrangement with Mackintosh. The only way he will increase his investment, without assuming control of the company, is if he becomes an extended part of our family.'

'And that means serving me up to him like a Christmas present!'

'It means doing what has to be done, keeping our partnership both equal and secure.'

Ariette wrung her hands and gnashed her teeth. 'It isn't fair to ask this of me.'

'No, it isn't,' Brock admitted. 'But your brothers both left home to find their fortunes back East and your sister, Victoria, is married and has two children. There's only you to maintain our family's effective partnership.'

'There must be other men of means about, someone who can contribute the financial aid we need, a person closer to my own age.'

'There's no time. My back is against the wall. This is the only option open to us.'

Ariette ducked her head, agonizing at the helplessness of her situation. 'But, Father . . . how do I bear the shame of having to allow a stranger, an old man to—' she couldn't finish.

'I'm sure you will find Big Mack – that's what most people call him – a man you can admire, respect, and even love one day. He is a gentleman, a most jovial fellow, and he looks much younger than his years.'

'Dare I ask how old he is?'

'He is a few years younger than me,' Brock admitted uncomfortably. 'He was married as a young man but his wife died of fever and he's been alone ever since. He is an able provider, a solid businessman, and I'm sure he will be a fine husband.'

'And the *father* of our children,' she put in sourly. Then added: 'Until he dies of old age five or ten years from now.'

'None of us have a guarantee when it comes to age. Aunt Mabel turned eighty last year and is still in fine health.'

'Yes, but Uncle George died when I was little. What kind of life has Mabel had, living alone all these years?'

'Her daughter's family moved in and is living with her,' he countered. 'She isn't alone.'

'She isn't with the man she loved either.'

Brock had discussed it as much as he was going to. 'You can go shopping with your mother and buy some clothes and things you might need. Anything else, I'm sure Mackintosh will provide for you.'

Ariette realized arguing would get her nothing. Resigned to her dreaded fate, she asked: 'Will you and Mother be coming to the wedding?'

'The marriage won't be much of a ceremony, I'm afraid. They have a parson in Lost Bend. That's the closest town to the end of the tracks. Your union with Big Mack is more of a business transaction than a wedding. I'm sorry, but that's the way it is.'

Ariette whirled about, blinded by tears, and rushed from the office. She slammed the door behind her and paused to put a hanky to her eyes. Amanda, their family housekeeper, had been waiting in the secretary's office. It wasn't a good idea for a proper young lady to be alone on the streets of Cheyenne, so she had attended her to the meeting and waited to escort her home.

'Mr Ekhard would not relent?' the woman asked gently.

'Not in the slightest,' Ariette told her, dabbing at the troublesome and wasted tears. 'I am to ready myself for a journey to the end of the tracks.'

'You're not making the trip all alone?'

Ariette simmered down enough to sigh. 'I'm sure Father will provide a bodyguard. He would be most disconcerted if I were to get lost along the way.'

'Oh, joy,' Amanda said critically, not bothering to hide her dismay. 'Indenture you for life to an older man out in the middle of . . . where are you going?'

Ariette heaved a sigh of resignation. 'Some place near a town called Lost Bend, in Wyoming. I'll go as far as the nearest way station and be met there and transported to the end of the rails.'

'I'm so sorry, dear. I know this isn't the life you dreamed of when we moved this far west.'

'It's my duty, my curse, for being an Ekhard.'

CHAPTER TWO

Bolt entered the saloon at Deek's side. The place was mostly empty at this early hour, but a couple of men were playing cards at a table in the corner and three more were standing at the bar. As his eyes adjusted to the dark interior, he recognized the trio as the Voight brothers. Sam and Clyde each wore a single gun, while Rich – he liked to think of himself as a bad man with a gun – wore a double-rig, with shiny pearl-handled guns.

'I'm callin' you out, Sam Voight!' Deek announced loudly, standing with the shotgun muzzles pointed at the floor. 'You can step into the street or die where you stand. It's my sister's death I'm here to collect for.'

As one, the three men rotated about to face the newcomers. Bolt didn't hesitate, but quickly drew his gun. He held both Rich and Clyde under its muzzle.

'It's a square fight this man is asking for,' he said. 'I aim to keep it that way.' He gave a tip of his head.

'You two move out of the way and there'll be no need for any extra gunplay.'

Rich snorted like a jackass that had inhaled a feather up its nose. 'Who the hell do you think you are – Wild Bill Hickok?'

The bartender hurried to the end of the bar, out of the line of fire. At the same time the card players left the table, tipping over their chairs and scampering off as if a skunk had jumped up on the tabletop.

'This is between Sam and his brother-in-law,' Bolt repeated. 'Drop your hardware and step aside.'

Rich elbowed Clyde. 'What do you think?' he asked. 'Want to take him?'

'Damn, Rich!' his brother replied. 'The muzzle of his Colt pointed right at my chest. I reckon I'll toss my iron.'

'Do as he says,' Sam instructed his kin smugly. 'I can handle this.'

Rich and Clyde both unhitched their belts and let the holsters and guns drop to the floor. Then they moved a few feet away from Sam. Bolt matched their move, keeping his gun aimed at the two. That was when the world ceased turning.

The buzzing of a nearby fly was the only sound in the room. Five men stood waiting, wary of each breath, eyes unblinking, watching intently, waiting for the fatal outcome. Who would be walking out of the saloon, and who would be carried out?

Sam's hand flashed downward for his pistol. . . .

Deek went into action at the same time, swinging

16

his scatter-gun around while thumbing back the twin hammers. The blast from his shotgun came a microsecond before Sam managed to get off his own shot.

The twin loads of buckshot propelled the wife-killer backwards. He banged into the gamblers' table and both he and the table crashed to the floor.

The two brothers started forward, but Bolt stopped them with, 'Hold it!' He waved them back a step and went over to check on Sam himself. There was no need to search for a pulse; Sam was dead. He removed the gun that was lying next to the body and stood up.

'This is the end of it,' he said to the two Voight boys. 'Sam killed this man's sister and now he's paid the price. The game is even and done with.'

'You jaw all you want,' Rich sneered. 'We'll be comin' for you two.'

Bolt swung both guns around and put the brothers under the muzzles. 'If you're going to push this, I can end it for you right here.'

Clyde shook his head. 'No, mister,' he said fearfully. 'We ain't lookin' for no more trouble.'

'How about it?' Bolt asked Rich. 'You want to strap on your hog-leg and have a go? Or do we walk away and let you bury your no-good, wife-murdering brother?'

The man glanced at Sam's dead body. There was hateful malice in his eyes, but he controlled his voice when he spoke.

'You've got the high hand this time, mister. We'll

tend to our brother.' Then, in a cooler tone, 'But I wouldn't stick around town if I were you.'

'Sounds like good advice,' Bolt replied. 'I'll leave your guns at the general store.'

Rich and Clyde moved over to their fallen brother, while Bolt scooped up the guns and left the saloon. Deek followed him wordlessly. He waited while the guns and holsters were deposited with the storekeeper and Bolt had cleared his things out of his room. It wasn't until they were walking to the stable that he finally cleared his throat.

'I'm right sorry to have pulled you into this.'

'I was leaving today anyway.'

'Those two will come looking for us,' Deek said.

'Probably with several of their friends and relatives,' Bolt agreed. 'I've seen old man Voight in town a time or two. He's one of those fathers who raises his sons to be as mean and nasty as he is himself. I've heard he has a brother somewhere near by, but I've never seen him or his family.'

'I still feel bad about you being pulled into this. If those fellas up and kill you, it'll be on my conscience.'

'Sam killed your sister, Deek. That's enough for me to stand at your side. You don't owe me anything.'

'You're a good man, Bolt.'

'Where you headed now?' Bolt asked, while saddling up his horse.

'Dunno. I kind of left everything behind.' He shrugged. 'I knew Sam had a tough family; I didn't

18

really figure I'd live through the fight.'

'How do you feel about working for the railroad?'

'Digging rock and stringing rail?' Deek winced. 'I'm not sure I'm cut out for that kind of labor. Pounding a nail with a hammer is much easier work than driving spikes and laying railroad ties.'

'I might get you something a little less taxing, if you can read and write.'

'That much I can do.'

'Then you're welcome to come along to the end of the tracks with me. I'll speak to my boss on your behalf. He said he would need me for a special job in a few days. If he takes a liking to you, maybe you can tag along.'

'Won't be out anything but the ride if he says no,' Deek replied. 'Like I said, I've nowhere else to go.'

Sam's father stood with his head lowered, but he was not listening to the words being said over his son's grave. He was consumed by a raging fire of anger that completely overwhelmed his grief. Someone had dared kill one of his family. His brother Ethan moved over to stand at his side.

'Got here a little late, but we made it,' he said, patting Mortimer on the shoulder. 'I'm durn sorry about Sam.'

'Shotgun blast,' Mortimer told him. 'He was gunned down like a wild animal – had no chance atall. It was Nancy's good-for-nothing brother.' He swore savagely. 'She made Sam's life miserable, nagging him constantly about having to do the cooking, cleaning and laundry for the four of us. Finally get rid of her and her brother arrives to murder Sam!'

'Don't know why Sam ever married that gal,' Ethan said. 'This ain't no place to be raising a family.'

Mortimer groaned. 'I think he figured to give me a grandson. He always talked about how he would raise his boys to walk tall and not take anything from anyone.' Another profanity. 'And he brought home a barren woman who couldn't even do that!'

Ethan waited a few seconds, but Mortimer had finished cursing his daughter-in-law. Turning to the task ahead, he said: 'Clyde was saying a second jasper held him and Rich under his gun while Sam was being kilt.'

'Yeah, the guy was around town for a few days before the killing. He works for the railroad. Deacon Johnston left town with him.'

'Then you know where to find him?'

Mortimer looked at Ethan and nodded to a man standing a short way off. 'That fellow knows where to find him, but he has an offer for how we can make a pile of money first. I ain't heard him out yet, but we did a job with him and a couple of his pals a year or so back.'

'Sounds promising.'

'You bring your boys?'

'Yep, you 'member Myra Ann done got herself married a few months back. With Joab sitting in the Colorado pen for another few years and Beth planted in the family cemetery, it's only the three of us now.'

'Beth was a good woman,' Mortimer avowed. 'She gave you four kids that reached adulthood. My Gloria was the same, 'cepting our girl died of fever as a child.'

'I've been thinking of moving over this way,' Ethan ventured. 'Might get a piece of land next to yourn. The boys need something to keep them out of trouble. Neither one much favors the idea of working for wages.'

'We could make a go of the ranch,' Mortimer told him. 'With the money this railroad man is promising, we could get ourselves a fair-sized stake.'

'Me and the boys are ready,' Ethan advised. 'Our family ain't made much money from catching and breaking wild horses. It's been a chore to keep bread on the table.'

'We're in about the same shape. Lately, we've been getting by on credit and barter in town.' He snorted belligerently. 'Nobody messed with me or my boys till Sam's brother-in-law showed up.'

'Let's have a talk with your railroad contact. Maybe there's a way to earn some money and get even with those two *hombres* who murdered Sam.'

Mortimer bobbed his head. 'We'll listen and see what he has to say. If he's got a workable plan, it might be good way for us to start a ranch together.'

'I'll drink to that!'

Ariette bounced from the dip in the road, groaned

21

from the hard jolt and frowned at her taciturn, six-foot-tall, bodyguard. Montague's face resembled a punching bag – aptly so, because he had done quite a bit of boxing for money. He often accompanied her father, but this was the first time he had been assigned to protect Ariette.

'Would you please tell the driver to watch where he's going!' she complained. 'I don't wish to arrive looking like I've been dragged through a briar patch!'

'Yes, ma'am,' Montague said. It was the first time he had put together two words – or what passed for words in his limited vocabulary.

He rotated his 200-pound frame, pulled aside the dust curtain, and stuck his head out of the stage window.

'Hey! Feather-brain!' he bellowed. 'Watch where you're going!'

But the driver shouted at the team to go faster. It seemed the coach was flying down the dirty, rutted trail.

'Get down!' the man handling the reins shouted to Montague.

Montague pulled his head back inside the coach as there came the sound of a gunshot. It sounded very close!

'What on earth. . . ?' Ariette cried.

'Trouble!' The man stated the obvious.

They plunged through a washed-out section of trail and bounced along at breakneck speed. Both of them clung to the doorstraps to keep from being tossed about like a pair of rubber balls.

More gunfire! A cry of pain!

The erratic stage violently hit something and the world turned askew.

Ariette let go of the strap and threw up her arms defensively as her escort flew across the coach interior and landed on top of her. The wind was knocked from her lungs, and she was crushed under the man's weight as the stage plowed to a complete stop, lying on its side.

Dust boiled about the interior of the coach. Ariette heard a scraping sound as someone climbed up on the side of the stage. The door was suddenly lifted open and the sunlight shone brightly through the opening. Although dazed and half-suffocated by Montague's weight, Ariette looked around his shoulder to see the blurred image of a man standing there. He had a gun aimed at them. Before she could utter a sound, he pulled the trigger!

Montague, who had been attempting to lift himself up, grunted and sagged heavily against Ariette. She lacked the breath to scream, but attempted to squirm deeper beneath her guard's body for protection. A second look at the shooter caused Ariette to gasp in horror. He was preparing to climb through the open door!

CHAPTER THREE

'First week on the job and I'm riding out to help you play nursemaid to some spoiled brat,' Deek said drily. 'I never suspected life would be so gloriously satisfying working for the railroad.'

'It's a business-arranged marriage,' Bolt explained, as they rode side-by-side over a slight rise. 'Big Mack is a widower and has money – his partner in this railroad venture is a man named Ekhard, and he has a grown daughter. Ekhard ran out of money, so this is his way of maintaining a half-interest in the line.'

'Mr Mackintosh is rather seasoned,' Deek pointed out. 'Got to wonder how eager this young bride will be to marry a man who's on the shy side of fifty.'

'Not my concern. I'm Mack's lead foreman, which means I don't question his orders. There's supposed to be a team and buggy waiting for us at the way station.'

'And I'm riding with you because . . . I'm what?'

He squinted at Bolt. 'What title did you give me?'

'It's an assistant foreman job: timekeeper and paymaster. . . .' he grinned and added: 'horse-tender, fire-builder, cook, and jack of all trades. Better than driving railroad spikes ten hours a day, don't you think?'

'If you say so. I'm obliged for the chance. . . .'

The sound of distant gunfire caused them both to pull back on the reins of their mounts. With the rolling terrain, they could see nothing beyond the next hill.

'Indians?'

'Could be,' Bolt said. 'Doesn't really matter. It's coming from the main road, and it's between town and the way station. Let's check it out.'

The two of them put their horses into a run and climbed the rise in front of them. As the road came into view Bolt spotted the stage. It was lying on its side with dust still boiling about. The team had stopped, still harnessed to the coach. A body was lying a few feet from the driver's box and three riders had surrounded the overturned rig.

Bolt dug his heels into his steed's ribs while pulling his Winchester from its boot. He jacked a shell into the chamber as they drew to within a couple hundred yards. Even as he lifted the rifle with his right hand and pressed the butt against his shoulder, he saw one of the men climb atop the stage.

Still too far to make out the man's face, or for a good shot, he could only urge more speed from his mount. The fellow lifted the door, but this wasn't a normal robbery: the bandit fired into the coach.

Bolt could wait no longer. Taking quick aim, he attempted to hit the target from the back of his running horse. The bullet smacked into the stage's door, missing the shooter by inches. It was close enough; it caused the man to jump back in surprise and he let the door slam shut. He scrambled off the coach and quickly mounted his horse.

Meanwhile the other two bandits began to fire at Bolt, but they were using handguns and were still out of range. Bolt cocked and fired a second time, boring down on them at less than a hundred yards. This time he scored a hit, knocking the attacker who had been atop the coach from his horse.

Deek had his shotgun out and was also going full out. He needed only a few more yards to be in range. However, the two remaining bandits had no stomach for a fight. They turned their horses and raced off through the sage, lying low over the necks of their animals to present the smallest of targets.

Bolt let them go, worried someone might be gravely wounded inside the stage. As he pulled back his galloping horse a hurried glance told him the driver was unconscious or dead. The man he had shot also looked primed for a grave.

'Check those two,' he told Deek, as they pulled up at the scene.

He neck-reined his horse over next to the coach, climbed atop the saddle and leapt upon the stage.

Then he grabbed the handle and started to lift the door. . . .

A bullet tore through the canvas curtain on the window, barely missing his head. Bolt fell back on to his heels and shouted: 'Hold it! We drove off the bandits. We're here to help!'

No word came from inside, so he eased the door open carefully. 'Hello?' he asked, before risking a peek inside.

'My bodyguard has been shot,' a woman's voice reached his ears. 'He's. . . .' she uttered an unfeminine grunt. 'He's on top of me. I can't get out from under him or see how badly he's hurt.'

Bolt leaned over and looked into the dark interior. All he could see of the female was her head and one hand – which still held a pistol.

Laying the door flat, in the open position, Bolt lowered himself into the coach. He managed to straddle both the girl and the gunshot man as he climbed down next to them both. A quick examination was enough to see the bodyguard was dead.

'You hit?' he asked the young lady.

'No,' she said, tossing the gun aside. He saw the girl had acquired the weapon from the dead man, as his holster was empty. 'That crazy road agent – I think he was going to kill me!'

'Lucky we heard the shooting. I managed to get off a shot at him before he could finish whatever he had in mind. I'm sorry we weren't able to save your hired man.'

'This is insane!' she declared. 'They didn't even

offer us a chance to surrender.'

'They were sure enough cold-blooded killers.' Bolt remarked, while he found places to brace his feet. He grunted from the effort to move the corpse to one side. Then he took hold of the girl's wrists and lifted her up to a standing position. Placing his hands at her waist, he hefted her up through the coach opening. She used both hands to help lift herself and he caught hold of her ankles and steadied her until she could sit on the stage and swing her legs around. He followed her up and helped lower her to where she could slide down off the overturned coach. Deek moved over to aid the process, catching her and easing her to the ground. He stepped away at once.

'Both men are dead,' he informed Bolt as he dropped to the ground next to them. 'No papers on the masked man, but he has an unusual mouth – you know, what they call a hare-lip?'

'Should make identifying him easier,' Bolt acknowledged.

'But why attack us?' the girl asked, fussing to tuck a lock of raven-black hair into the bun at the back of her head. 'I'm not carrying any money. And why kill my bodyguard?'

'The one who shot into the coach looked as if he was about to climb inside,' Bolt said. 'It could be that he was going to grab you, rather than kill you. Had he wanted you dead, he could have kept shooting.'

The girl pulled a face at the observation. 'Why

would he want to kidnap me?'

Bolt considered that for a moment. 'You're Ariette Ekhard, aren't you.'

It wasn't a question, so the lady only tipped her head forward in an affirmative gesture.

'You're supposed to marry Big Mack . . . uh, Mr Mackintosh,' he continued.

'And someone wants me dead because of my father's arrangement with Mr Mackintosh?'

Bolt didn't answer her but Deek spoke up. 'You think Proctor is behind this?'

'No, Proctor isn't a criminal. He wouldn't sanction murder and kidnapping.'

'You told me this here line meant a great deal of money,' Deek argued. 'Greed knows no bounds and has no conscience. A kidnapping would give him the upper hand.'

'That's ridiculous!' Ariette cried. 'I didn't want this marriage. I'm not a part of this lunatic competition!'

'Might not be your idea, but you're involved,' Bolt advised her. 'The rail to Cedar Flats has to go through Breakneck Pass. It's the shortest route by nearly forty miles, but it's only wide enough for one set of tracks.'

'I don't understand.'

'Proctor's railroad line is coming from the west and Mackintosh has his rails coming from the east. Whoever gets to the pass first will surely reach Cedar Flats well ahead of the other. That means a big bonus from the government and control of the mail

– which is a sizable contract. At the moment, we are several miles ahead of Proctor and should easily reach the pass first.' He lifted a hand in a helpless gesture. 'However, Mackintosh and your father are equal partners and this work is expensive. Mack told me you were to marry him because your father was out of money, but wanted to remain a full partner. That means Mack is putting up a lot of extra cash to finish this on his own.'

'Yes, lucky me,' Ariette said in a caustic tone of voice. 'I'm collateral for my father's lack of funds.' Then, she added with obvious disgust: 'My life and worth have been reduced to a quaint barter system among railroad barons.'

'I'm sorry, miss,' Bolt sympathized, 'but that's how the deal plays out.'

Ariette put her hands on her hips and stared out over the expanse of sparsely covered sage land-scape. 'What now?'

'We'll have to tip the stage back on to its wheels and take it to the station. There's a buckboard waiting for the rest of the trip to the end of the line. That's where they are laying track. Mack has a special car there. It's as luxurious as a fancy hotel, complete with a housekeeper who also cooks. I'm sure you'll be comfortable.'

'I can hardly wait,' Ariette muttered sarcastically.

It took Bolt and Deek several hours to get the stage on its wheels and make enough repairs for it to roll along the dirt road. One of the horses on the team had been dragged down when the coach over-turned. He had a fairly bad limp, so he was attached behind the stage along with the other three mounts.

For travel, Bolt put the three bodies in the boot and he was the one to drive. Deek had never handled a team before, so he rode up on the box next to Bolt. Ariette had the inside of the coach to herself.

The way station was in the middle of miles and miles of nothingness, the spot chosen because it was a place that had water year round. Often used for overnight travelers, the stationer had built a bunkhouse for guests. It was mostly sod, with just enough logs and timber to make the interior six foot high.

It was dusk when the stage limped into the yard. A man and a teenage boy came out of the main house to greet them and see why they were running so late. Bolt explained the attack, then asked about overnight arrangements for the three of them.

'Ma has a kettle of stew simmering,' the stationer replied. 'I'll have her set out plates for you. Soon as we put the animals up I'll show you where you can bunk. Not much privacy for a lady, but we do have a blanket we can hook to a couple of nails to section off a bed in one corner of the guest quarters.'

'I'm sure that will do. We will be leaving in the morning for the end of the tracks.'

'We'll stable your three animals,' their host observed. 'A buckboard was delivered two days back, along with a two-horse team. They will be

31

ready for the trip.'

'The extra mount belongs to the bandit in the boot,' Bolt advised him.

'We'll put Duffy – that's the only name I knew the driver by – we'll put him and the lady's companion in the coach. We can leave the murdering skunk in the boot. I'll take the stage back to Lost Bend myself. That's where I have to go to telegraph for a new driver and any repair items the stage requires.'

'I'd appreciate you sending a wire to Mr Ekhard and let him know what happened to his hired man.'

'Can do, sonny. Just write down what you want to say and I'll have it put over the wire.'

'Guess that catches us up to our present situation,' Bolt approved. 'I'll give you a hand with the horses and the bodies.'

'Let's get to it,' the station manager said.

Ariette was stiff and sore, with a number of bumps and bruises caused when the coach flipped on its side. The weight of Montague landing on top of her had added to her minor injuries, but his body had protected her from being shot. Fortunately, the bullet that hit him had been at enough of an angle to miss her when it passed through him.

Ariette entered the way station and saw the station keeper's wife – Mexican or Indian, Ariette didn't know which. There was a single long table in the middle of the room, with a bench for sitting on either side. It looked big enough to handle ten or twelve people at one time. The woman didn't speak a word, but pointed and grunted to the rear door.

Ariette went that direction; it led out to a small back porch. She discovered a bar of lye soap, a pan of water, and a threadbare towel that had long since lost any of its original color. Although it had begun to shred from overuse, the cloth was moderately clean. She was able to wash her face and hands, tidy the strands of hair back in place with hairpins, then clean a few of the red stains from the front of her dress. She could not suppress a shiver of revulsion, knowing it was the life blood of a man who had died protecting her, a reticent individual she had barely known.

By the time she re-entered the dining portion of the main room, eating utensils and several tin plates had been set upon the table. There was a pot of stew, ready for dishing up, and empty cups at each setting. A pot of coffee had been placed next to the kettle of stew, along with a jug of water. Even as she took a seat the woman brought over a loaf of bread. She didn't ask if Ariette wanted any, but broke off a chunk and set it next to her plate.

'Thank you,' Ariette said. 'It looks delectable.'

The lady paused to look at her and shook her head. 'You not belong here.'

Ariette arched her brows in surprise. 'Excuse me?'

'You lady,' the woman firmly attested. 'No lady come this place.'

'It wasn't by choice I assure you,' Ariette responded candidly. 'How do you stand living so far from civilization?'

With a shrug, 'Woman go where her man take her.'

Ariette smiled. 'I understand. It's why I'm here, too. My father is forcing me to marry a railroad tycoon.'

The woman grunted. 'Same for white lady as for Indian: men order, we go.'

There was no further talk. Deek came through the door and displayed a wide, infectious grin.

'Hot dang! Supper's on the table! My shirt buttons have been pressing against my backbone for the last hour.'

He came over and started to sit down opposite Ariette. She glanced at his blackened hands from working on the coach and riding all day and remarked, 'There's a place to wash just out the back door.'

Deek stopped halfway to sitting down on the bench. He stared at his grimy paws and laughed. 'Durned if being empty-bellied didn't trump my civilized manners. I plumb forgot all about washing.'

He excused himself and hurried out the back door. Bolt didn't show for a few minutes. When he did join them, however, he had taken time to clean up and looked much more a gentleman. Ariette guessed he must have washed at one of the watering troughs as his sleeves were damp, along with the collar of his shirt.

It was the first time Ariette had taken a good look at him. The man was a little above average height, with pleasant features and steady-going dark eyes. He was brawny in appearance without being excessively muscular. He removed his hat to reveal well-groomed, dusty-brown colored hair that tended to curl slightly from his hat. Lissome in his movements, he took the place-setting furthermost from her. She wondered if it was shyness or something else. After he served up a portion of stew on to his plate, he glanced in her direction – not a look or acknowledgment, but a covert peek, as if he was unwilling to gaze directly at her.

'Been a heck of a day,' Deek spoke up upon returning to the room. He didn't avoid Ariette, once more sitting down on the opposite side of the table. Another automatic smile curled his lips. 'Bet this is a trip you'll never forget, young lady.'

'I'm sure I won't,' Ariette answered back.

'Me and Bolt will do some investigating, once we get you to the end of the tracks. We'll find out who is behind the attack.'

'What can you do about it?' she asked. 'I mean, there isn't any law out here, is there?'

'Bolt claims we can call in the army if it comes to a major fight. The soldiers are supposed to protect the railroaders. The laying of track is progress for the entire country: more food, good jobs, land for settlers, civilization and growth. Yes sir, this here country will one day be able to feed the world.'

'That's a rather grandiose statement.'

Deek laughed. 'Yeah, I 'spect I sometimes get caught up with a notion. But we've put the war behind us and got nothing but progress, invention and expansion ahead. Look how much we've done in the short time we've been on this here continent. The limits are boundless.'

'If you say so.'

He took a bite of stew and chewed thoughtfully for a moment. 'What about you, ma'am?' he asked. 'Is this the fulfillment of your dreams, to marry a railroad king?'

'As I told Mr Bolt, this wasn't my idea. My father is using me as collateral so he can remain a full partner with Mr Mackintosh.'

'Sorry,' said Deek. 'I do remember you saying as much. I was so busy wondering what kind of war I'd stepped into, the words didn't register in my brain.'

'How did you come to be working with Mr Bolt?'

'Uh, I ain't rightly sure if Bolt is his first, last, or even his real name,' Deek said. 'Out in this wilderness, a good many men only go by a nickname.'

Brazenly, Ariette stared down the table at Bolt. He gave no indication he had been listening to their conversation, but she was positive he had heard every word.

'Well?' she asked him directly. 'Are you Mr Bolt, or are you one of the mysterious men of the West who doesn't have a last name?'

'Bolt is what everyone calls me – no mister, just Bolt.'

'Very well, *Bolt*,' she said flippantly. 'What is your role in my planned marital subjugation?'

36

He flinched, as if her words stung, but his answer was clear and simple. 'I work for Big Mack.'

'Yes, I gathered as much from the fact you were to meet and escort me to him.' She bore into him with a steady perusal. 'I was curious as to your title, your job description, your position with the company.'

'Senior foreman, track manager and head of security,' he answered.

'Sounds as if you do about everything. Does Mr Mackintosh supervise and oversee the railroad workers?'

'Mack is the boss.' Bolt dismissed the question.

Ariette grew impatient. 'Why do you refuse to look at me? It lacks proper etiquette to not address a lady to her face.'

Bolt swallowed the bite of food he'd been chewing and rotated enough to meet her challenge. For a moment he merely studied her. Actually, his examination was as intense as if she were the most expensive horse at an auction. He didn't just look at her, he scrutinized her every strand of hair, each individual eyelash, her lips, nose and chin, and then he dismantled her sturdy veneer with a thoroughness that passed beyond her return gaze and invaded the furthermost regions of her mind.

Ariette drew back defensively, cowed and intimidated by such a candid appraisal. Meekly, she could only shut him out by shielding her eyes with lowered lids. The brief encounter caused a hot flush that warmed her entire being and surely suffused color

37

to her cheeks. Never had a man unsettled her so completely by simply staring into her eyes.

'You were saying?' he queried curtly.

Struggling to recover, Ariette coughed ignominiously and put her hankie to her mouth. After a moment, she squeaked out: 'Oh, that last bite went down the wrong way.'

'I beg your pardon for ignoring you, Miss Ekhard,' Bolt apologized to relieve the tension between them. 'I haven't been in the presence of a genteel and beautiful lady, such as yourself, for a very long time. A man loses a sense of proper conduct being so far from civilization.'

'Of course,' she replied, battling to regain her decorum. 'It's just that ... well, you saved my life. I've been remiss in not expressing my gratitude. After all,' she hurried to add, 'it isn't your fault I'm being forced into a marriage.'

'Perhaps not, Miss Ekhard, but it goes against the grain to be a part of your unhappy situation. I don't happen to believe in arranged weddings.'

'Oh? Do you have such a high code of ethics?'

'Lady,' Deek intervened before Bolt could offer a reply. 'The man sitting at the end of the table risked his life to see that I had a fair chance to deal with the man who killed my sister.' He put on a stern frown. 'And Bolt didn't know me from a drifting tumbleweed.'

Ariette did not hide her surprise, staring in awe at Deek.

'Yep,' he rushed forth with his story, 'Bolt seen I

was primed to fight and knew I didn't have so much as a prayer against three men. He stood up with me and held off the man's two brothers, while me and the murdering scum settled our differences.' He did not hide his admiration for Bolt. 'You couldn't find a more honorable man if you were to search for a thousand miles around.'

Ariette saw Bolt swallow hard, mortified by the praise. In a display of humility, he shook his head.

'Deek,' he said, 'You've a knack for exaggeration that could turn a cow chip into a birthday cake. All I did was give you a fighting chance. If you had hesitated for even a split second, you'd be lying in a grave, instead of bragging on me.'

'Make slight of it if you've a mind to, Bolt. But I owe you my life, and you gave me a job to boot. I aim to pay you back one day.'

'I hired you because of your character, Deek,' Bolt said. 'You don't owe me anything for standing at your side. I'd have done that for anyone who had a just cause.'

Both men had said their piece and now returned to eating. Ariette acquired a new attitude about Bolt . . . and Deek. Seldom had she encountered a pair with such virtuous and admirable characteristics.

Returning to her plate, she found a bite or two of potato that was edible. The chunks of meat in the stew were tough enough to have come from between the horns of a retired bull, so she soaked the bread in the gravy and used it to satisfy her hunger. She needed to keep up her strength for whatever lay ahead. And, after giving it a lot of thought, she had decided not to throw her life away without a fight.

CHAPTER FOUR

Sirus Proctor listened until his son had finished giving him an update of events. Then he banged his fist on his desk and his face darkened with anger and frustration. 'When did this happen?'

'Earlier today. There were three men – one of them was the harelip, Jack Rutledge.'

Sirus scowled at the news. 'That fellow who used to deliver our supplies?'

'Yep. He and a couple others tried to kidnap the girl – Mack's bride-to-be.'

'For the love of . . .' Sirus cursed. 'Mack is going to think we're behind this.'

'Maybe not. Bolterfeld and another man showed up and killed Jack. The other two outlaws ran like a couple of mice in a house full of cats. We've no connection to those men.'

'Ransom, you think?'

'Has to be. That girl is the only way Ekhard can remain an equal partner with Mack. She would be worth a small fortune.'

Sirus gave a bob of his head. 'Was the girl injured?'

'No, she and Bolt, along with another guy from the railroad, are at the way station.'

'How did you find all this out?'

'One of the boys was there to meet the stage and pick up any mail that was coming our way.'

'Then nothing has changed concerning Mack's situation.'

'Nothing, Pa. We're still running almost two weeks behind their crew. Unless something else happens, they are going to reach the pass well ahead of us.'

Proctor stared off into space, raking his brain for an idea or alternative. He had never liked defeat. He had learned the ethics of big business – lie, cheat or steal to beat the competition. Plus, winning this race was also about saving a pile of money and making even more. If Mackintosh managed to reach the main line first, he would get the mail contract and have first chance to make the connection at the proposed stockyards. That left almost nothing for Proctor's line, other than transport west. Arriving second meant several years of rail service would be necessary to recoup the amount of money he had invested in this spur.

'Too bad the outlaw plan didn't work,' Rip said. 'A kidnapping might have slowed down Mack's crew. If he had sent his men searching the hills, we might have gained a few days on them.'

'No, son,' Sirus said. 'I would love to beat

Mackintosh, but we got started too late. He got the jump on us and was able to find ways to shorten the route. We had to take a straight shot and then were held up by having to build trestles over two blasted washouts.'

'I still say we should have done a little sabotage to slow him down. One fake Indian raid would have disrupted them enough to set them back a week. That's about all we needed.'

'Mack would have found out we were behind it and retaliated,' Sirus countered. 'We would have both spent valuable time and money doing repairs, and we would still be a week behind them.'

'I'm just saying, it's a lot of money we stand to lose.'

'We can only keep pushing the men,' Sirus said. 'If we don't get some kind of break to close the gap between us, we will turn at the edge of the western hills and head for the main line.'

'Reckon that's all we can do, Pa. Hate to lose out on the race, but it don't appear humanly possible for us to beat Mack's crew.'

'Keep a sharp eye on Mackintosh; we need to know if anything develops. We've still got a few days before we reach the turning point.'

'Don't worry, Pa. I've got eyes all over Mack's camp. Anything happens, we'll know about it.'

The room had become quiet, other than for the deep, even breathing of the two men. Ariette waited a bit longer, making certain they were sleeping soundly. Then she eased out of bed and picked up her shoes. She had her purse and light jacket under her arm as she moved aside the blanket partition and tiptoed across the room in her bare feet.

The door had been left ajar as a sagging roof beam no longer allowed it to swing freely. Ariette nudged it open a few inches further and stepped into the adjoining room. She eased past the long table and benches, out through the front of the station and paused to put on her shoes.

'Goin' fer a walk?' a soft, youthful voice asked quietly.

Ariette's heart about exploded in her chest. She gasped, but stifled a cry of surprise. Quickly regaining her poise, she discovered the person speaking was the stationer's teenage boy.

'You work all day and then keep watch all night?' she asked, also in a hushed voice.

'Not usually, miss,' he replied, lowering his head bashfully. 'It's on account of them bandits attacking your stage. Pa thought someone ought to keep an eye open tonight.'

Ariette finished slipping on her shoes, then both she and the youth walked away from the building to keep anyone from overhearing their talking. When she reached the front of the barn she stopped and studied him. He was a gangly kid, long arms and legs, with large hands and a face like a pet dog, complete with large, gentle eyes and a soulful expression on his face. Ariette veered away from vanity, but knew she was above average in looks. A pretty girl

44

often promoted shyness from a young man. Many of them felt inadequate to associate with an attractive lady. It was an edge she chose to exploit.

'What's your name?' she asked.

'Lawrence Pine.' He displayed a self-conscious grin. 'Most everyone calls me Larry.'

'Larry, I need your help.'

'Me?' He did not hide his shock. 'But them two fellers you come with, they done saved you from them outlaw types. I reckon they'd be more help than me.'

'No,' she said quickly. 'It's something I have to do on my own.'

'What be you needing?'

'A saddled horse. I have to get away before those bad men come looking for me. I don't wish to have anyone else die on my behalf.'

'But it ain't safe for a woman to ride alone, not way out here.'

'I'll follow the road and return to Lost Bend. Once I'm there, I'll wire my father that I'm coming home. I'll take the stage to the train station and be gone before anyone is the wiser.'

'Pa is going to make the trip to town tomorrow. You can ride back with him.'

'*No*,' she said, a bit too sharply. She immediately recovered and repeated, 'No, Larry. No one can know where I've gone.' There was a near-full moon overhead, as well as a lamp burning inside the barn. There was enough light for Ariette to know that the boy could see her clearly. She put on her very best pout.

'Don't you see?' she appealed for cooperation and understanding. 'I don't wish to marry a man who is as old as my father. I want to be courted by someone closer to my own age . . .' she regarded him with a beguiling look. 'Someone more like you.'

Larry's mouth fell open to reveal a mouthful of teeth that looked like a long-neglected picket fence, with boards missing and a couple twisted or leaning in errant directions. He slowly closed his trap and his protruding Adam's apple rose sharply and then dropped with his audible gulp.

'Wa'al, sure,' he drawled supportively. 'I can sure enough understand where you're coming from.'

'Plus, I would feel terrible if the two men who rescued me were to be injured or killed while trying to protect me.' She put her free hand on Larry's arm. 'You will help me, won't you?'

Larry's face transformed into a determined mask. 'Whatever you want, miss,' he promised. 'I'll do whatever you want.'

Mortimer and his son, Clyde, were surprised to see Handy tightening the cinch on his saddle, his horse standing ready to ride. Handy heard their approach and grabbed for his gun – only to stop the motion when he recognized the two men.

'You're early,' he greeted the pair. 'Didn't expect any relief till after midnight.'

'Looks like you're in a hurry to get going.'

Handy laughed. 'You won't believe it, but the girl

46

just slipped away on her own. She's headed down the road for town.'

'What?' Mortimer stared off into the dark. 'She did what?'

'Yep. I waited to make sure no one was following her. She's alone all right.'

Mortimer chuckled. 'She doesn't have the stomach for this part of the country. I'd wager she's running back to town to contact Daddy.'

'I'll run her down long before she can reach Lost Bend.'

'After safely getting away from the attack on the coach, the silly heifer has played right into our hands.'

Handy mounted his horse. 'You can head on back home. Be less of a trail to follow if I grab her on my own.'

'Don't let her see your face,' Mortimer warned. 'Blindfold her right off. Once you've done your best to hide your tracks, make your way to our place.'

'Just the way we planned before those two rail-roaders interfered.'

'Best bet is to use the creek crossing – might throw off any pursuit.'

'That was my thinking as well.'

Mortimer chuckled. 'With luck, this will go smoother than the plan we had to start out with.'

'Yeah, that didn't work out so well for Jack.'

'Think you will have any trouble getting ahead of her?'

'A green rider, at night?' Handy snorted his

contempt. 'She will be riding slow and careful, following the winding road. I'll have her at the ranch
by sunup.'

Bolt heard the station manager get up and go out
well before first light. A few minutes later he was
able to discern the sound of the team pulling out
with the stagecoach. It made sense, as the trip to
Lost Bend took six hours with a fresh team. The stationer had to leave early if he wanted to get back
home before dark.

Although he was not able to go back to sleep, he
stayed in bed so as not to disturb the lady or Deek.
Wasn't much chance any movement would have
bothered Deek. Having slept in the same room with
him since their first meeting, he knew his friend was
one of those lucky fellows – oblivious to the world
and able to sleep through a herd of cattle stamped-
ing through the room. As for the girl, Bolt had
gotten a couple hours of solid sleep before he
began waking up to listen to the sounds in the
night. So far, Ariette hadn't made a peep.

Lying there, his mind's eye kept picturing the girl
– first, helpless and frantic, pinned under the
weight of her bodyguard. But then she had boldly
confronted him at the table . . . until he had shamed
her into ducking behind lowered eyelids. She was
the most desirable young lady he had ever met. The
brightness of her mahogany eyes was mesmerizing.
And her overall radiance and beauty would beckon
a sculpture to create a masterpiece. She was graceful,

ladylike, with slender, yet exciting lips which enticed him like no woman before, not even in his dreams. He had never coveted another man's wife, but he definitely coveted Mack's wife-to-be.

Daylight arrived an hour later. Bolt got up quietly and went outside to wash up and shave at the watering trough. He was toweling off when the boy – eyes red from being up most of the night – came to fetch him for breakfast.

'Everything quiet?' Bolt asked him.

'Wa'al,' the young man drawled in a hesitant tone of voice. 'I noticed one of the horses is gone.' The youth could not hide a flash of guilt before lowering his gaze. 'I ain't sure whose horse is missing, but it's one of the three you brought with you yesterday.'

Bolt swore under his breath and raced into the station. He rushed past the still slumbering Deek and threw aside the curtain that isolated the girl's bunk.

'The little fool! What was she thinking?'

'Huh?' Deek asked, sitting up. 'What's the matter, Bolt?'

'Miss Ekhard sneaked out during the night and stole a horse. She must be heading for town.'

'Why would she do that?'

'Because she doesn't want to marry Mack.'

Deek pulled on his boots and grabbed his hat. 'We'd best get after her.'

'Breakfast is on the table,' the boy told them, having followed Bolt into the room. 'You might want to grab a bite to eat before you leave.'

49

'Did you see her?' Deek asked the young man. 'Weren't you supposed to be keeping watch?'

'I must have dozed off,' Larry said lamely, obviously lying.

Bolt didn't question him further. Under the same circumstances, he would have probably done whatever a stunning young woman like Ariette asked of him. He didn't fault the boy for being susceptible to the lady's charms.

'We'll eat a few bites, while you go out and saddle the two remaining horses.'

'Sure,' the kid said eagerly. 'I'll have them ready for you in two shakes of a calf's tail!'

'Tending a woman is like fishing with worn-out string,' Deek complained. 'You get a nice one on the line, get it almost to shore, and – snap! the line breaks.'

Ariette trembled uncontrollably, terrified as to what was happening. Strong hands gripped her waist and she was pulled down from her horse. As her feet touched the ground she was quickly guided a few steps into some kind of building. With a blindfold tightly in place, she could only see the toes of her own shoes. Her hands were also tied behind her, so tightly bound that her fingers had become numb. Dreadfully afraid, her heart hammered violently against her chest, while each breath took a tremendous effort to bring forth. Never had she felt such darkness, such terror.

'Here she is,' announced the man who had taken

her by surprise at the creek crossing. 'Didn't make it here before daylight, but there ain't nary a soul out moving about yet.'

'You did good. Everything is in place,' said a second man. 'We clear on the deal?'

The question must have been asked of a third man. His voice was more gruff. 'We'll do it the way you outlined,' he replied. 'The letter you had us write is ready and waiting for when the general store opens.'

'Shouldn't be anyone snooping around this far from town. We just have to keep her pinned up for the rest of the week and we'll all make a pile of money.'

'We'll handle our end of the deal,' came the crusty response. 'You tell the boss man that nothing better go wrong at his end.'

'He'll be by late today and discuss the details. This is going to work out for all of us. You'll see.'

Then it sounded as if two of the men left the room. Ariette felt the presence of the third man. He came to stand close enough for her to feel his breath against her face. It smelled of whiskey and cigar smoke.

'You do as you're told, woman.' It was the man with the harsh sounding voice. 'If you try anything cute, I'll take a belt to you. Do you understand what I'm saying?

Ariette bobbed her head.

'We're gonna leave you in this here shed. It's got no windows, and you're gonna put on that blindfold every time we open the door to feed you. So long as you never see anyone's face or learn where you are, you will live through this and be freed in a few days. You sneak one peek and I'll cut your throat. Do you understand?'

Ariette swallowed a lump of fear and again nodded her head.

The man took hold of her shoulders and roughly turned her around. He untied the knot on the rope about her wrists but left her lightly bound. Then he took a step back.

'You can remove the blindfold once the door is closed. There's water and some bread on the table. When we bring your supper, there will be a knock on the door and you will be told to cover your eyes.'

Ariette gave an obedient nod for the third time.

Her captor then went outside and the door scraped shut. A latch of some kind closed in place as Ariette worked the bonds loose. Once her hands were free, she removed the blindfold. Looking around, she discovered she was in a small outbuilding. A couple slivers of light came from under the eaves of the roof, but the steep slope of the ceiling did not allow for her to look outside. She spied a jug of water and part of a loaf of bread on a tin plate, both set on a stool – the only furniture in the room. A worn-thin quilt and single blanket were on the floor. All these were the entire contents of the room. As for the walls, they were wooden slabs with mortar between the cracks. There not so much as a knothole to peek through.

She removed her jacket and brushed off the riding-skirt she had donned while Larry had been saddling a horse for her. She had grabbed only her hairbrush, the few dollars she had tucked away and her jacket. The brush had fallen from her pocket during her struggle with the kidnapper, so she had only the clothes on her back.

'Good plan, Ariette,' she muttered to herself. 'You've managed to get yourself into a worse situation than marrying Tug Mackintosh.'

CHAPTER FIVE

Bolt and Deek took the shortest, fastest route to Lost Bend, but the girl had never arrived. Before they could sort out what to do next, the guy from the general store waved them over.

'I seen you come in,' he said to Bolt. 'I remember you saying you worked on the railroad.'

'Yes, for Tug Mackintosh.'

'Someone shoved this here letter under my door. Found it when I opened up for business. It don't have any kind of stamp, 'cause no one paid to send it. However, it's addressed to your boss.'

Bolt thanked the man and accepted the letter. Rather than put it aside to give to Mack, he tore it open. It took but a glance to tell him they had a major problem.

'Did I mention how this was just a simple escort job?' he asked Deek.

'Ah, no,' his pal groaned. 'Give me the bad news.'

'Someone has grabbed Miss Ekhard for ransom.'

Deek snorted. 'Well, that was real smart of her.

We risk our lives to save her from kidnappers, and she runs off on her own and ends up in their hands.'

Bolt folded the paper and stuck it back in the envelope. 'Ride as fast as you can to the end of the rails. Give this letter to Mack and then find the railroad scout, Scrapper Cobb.'

'He's the one who scouts for the surveyors ... right?'

Bolt gave an affirmative nod. 'The man's always bragging about his prowess during the last Indian war, enough to make your ears bleed. If he's half as good as he claims, we might have a chance of finding our missing bride.'

'Where do we meet?'

'Have Cobb start at the way station. The kid gave her my horse and that could help with the tracking. I had new shoes put on a week or so before I met you.'

'The stage and team will have destroyed most of the trail,' Deek pointed out.

'That's why I want Cobb to begin his search from that direction. I'll start from this end and see if I can pick up their sign. We should meet somewhere in the middle.'

Deek sighed. 'This here job is getting more demanding all the time.'

'Get going.'

Deek got his horse, climbed aboard, and lifted a hand in farewell. He left town at a lope. It would take him several hours to reach ;the rails and another couple to get the chores handled. Cobb would be lucky to get on the trail before sundown. If other travelers or wagons, besides the stagecoach and team, churned up the road, it would make it nearly impossible for anyone – no matter how good – to find the girl's trail.

Deek brought Mack Macintosh up to date on what had happened concerning Ariette, then handed him the hand-scribbled letter.

'This has to be Proctor's doing,' Mack bellowed. 'Who else would demand we stop laying rail until after the ransom is paid?'

'Bolt said I should find the tracker – Cobb? – and get him on the scent.'

'We're in luck there; he's in camp. He gave me the survey schematics of the proposed route through Breakneck Pass this morning. You should find him at the first sleeping-car.'

'You want me to pass along your suspicions to Bolt?' Deek wanted to know.

'No need,' Mack replied. 'He knows we are up against the wall on our timetable. If we shut down, Proctor will close the gap quickly. It wouldn't take but a few idle days and we would lose our advantage.'

'Are you going to halt the laying of tracks?'

Mack did some thinking. 'The men have been working long, hard shifts for the last six weeks. The kidnappers shouldn't expect me to stop in the middle of the day. I'll keep them working till the end of their shift. I can give the rail handlers and track workmen a three-day holiday. That should energize them for the final leg of the race. Plus, we can keep the freighters, graders and roustabouts working. Also, the men splitting and stacking rails. We'll use the time to get everything ready for when we start up again. There will be no delays for a hollow or wash to be filled in or leveled, no sitting back because we lack the ties or rails.'

'Then you're giving Bolt and me three days to find the girl and get her back,' Deek deduced.

'I will do everything in my power to keep that girl from harm, but I hate the idea of letting Proctor beat us through the pass. After the three days, I'll pay the ransom, if I can. If not. . . .' He made a face. 'Well, let's hope this is over by then.'

'You're the boss,' Deek said.

'I'll send a man to wire Ekhard and apprise him of the situation. You get Cobb tracking those kidnappers, and tell Bolt I'm counting on him.'

'You needn't worry about Bolt,' Deek replied. 'He's already looking for sign. It's a lucky break that Cobb isn't ten miles away. We should meet up with him sometime this afternoon.'

Mack gave a bob of his head and watched Deek hurry out of the railcar. Mrs Peterson, the widow who managed the cooking, cleaning, and kept the living quarters in order, came up behind him.

'The poor child,' she murmured. 'I'll bet she is frightened to death. First an attempt on her life, then she is kidnapped and held for ransom.'

'She ran away in the night,' Mack said, regret heavy in his voice. 'She ran away from a marriage to me.'

'She's what – twenty years old? The girl doesn't understand the realities of life yet.'

'I'm an old fool,' Mack said, 'more than twice her age. I don't blame her for running.'

'You are a decent and caring man,' Mrs Peterson argued. 'I'm sure, once Miss Ekhard gets to know you, she will come to cherish being your wife.'

Mack's shoulders sagged. 'It's just that I wanted children,' he admitted. 'Someone to leave my business to, a son to carry on my legacy. When my wife died I thought I would be denied those things. Brock offering Ariette as my bride – it was an answer to my prayers, a new contract on life.'

'I understand exactly how you feel,' the woman offered him comfort.

Mack regretted exposing his inner feelings so openly. Of course, Mrs Peterson knew about those things. She had lost her husband in the war and had mourned his passing until she was too along in years to bear children or start over. Mack had found her slaving away at a crossroads inn, working seven days a week, cooking and cleaning for dozens of guests, living in a storeroom, with not a dime in her pockets. He had offered her a position to cook for him and look after his house. When he went on the job, she traveled with him in his railroad car. It had been an acceptable living arrangement for them both.

'I apologize for airing my personal laundry,' he said uncomfortably. 'I must sound pitifully self-absorbed.'

The woman smiled. 'I'm the one who washes your personal laundry.'

The levity lightened his mood. 'You're a blessing to have around,' he said. 'I'm afraid I don't tell you that often enough.'

Instead of accepting the praise, Mrs Peterson said: 'It is natural that you should want a child, Mr Mackintosh. Most men wish to pass on their bloodline.'

He was warmed by her support. 'Two years you have been in my employ and you still call me Mr Macintosh.' She lowered her eyes respectfully and he continued: 'But, to tell the truth, it isn't only the desire for someone to carry my name, it's being able to hold a child of my own. I grew up an only child, lucky that my mother survived a difficult pregnancy. My father had a hardware business, leaving home early each morning and arriving late each night. Our one day together was Sunday, when we would go to church and have a family dinner. My father lived for Sundays all of his life, and died at forty-four. Mother, bless her heart, held on until I was old enough to be on my own.'

He paused, wondering why he was confiding in his servant. She had never told him of her lost dreams or feelings, never complained, even when he knew she was ailing from a headache or suffering from other ills. Still, he wanted her to know, to understand, even to empathize with him.

'I sold our house and the hardware business and invested in a new railroad. I won a contract for a three-hundred-mile stretch and it was a new beginning. Fifteen years later I joined up with Brock Ekhard and we started our own line. If we reach Cedar Creek first and tie into the main line, we will reap enough to be debt free and have our choice of a dozen new projects.'

'You don't think Mr Proctor is behind the kidnapping?' she asked. 'I mean, he surely wouldn't harm such an important young lady.'

'I intend to confront him about it, but I don't think he would risk something so criminal. However, the kidnappers did demand we stop laying rail until the ransom is paid. That strikes me as queer.'

'Do you think the kidnappers will get away with this; can they shut down the railroad until it's too late?'

'Not so long as Bolt is on the job,' Mack declared. 'I would never cast aspersions upon that man's heritage, but he could have been sired by a bloodhound. He has a determination and savvy few men possess. If I were to select one single thing that separates my railroaders and success against Proctor's line, it would be Bolterfeld. He will make the difference in who wins this race ... and he works for me!'

'He does seem extremely capable,' Mrs Peterson agreed. 'I'm sure he will find your missing bride.'

Mack studied her for a moment. Not a beautiful woman – the years had not been kind to her. Yet there was a competence and subdued pride about her demeanor. She had a subservient role in Mack's life, but had never complained. Perhaps three or four years younger than Mack, she had taken the grief and pain life delivered, yet always found the strength to smile and remain pleasant. Oftentimes he had wondered if she would consider being more than a servant.

The notion vanished at once. The age and gradual deterioration of the body did not control the mind. He felt as young as when he was twenty, just with a better sense of reality. His knowledge and experience made him a better choice for a husband than a more youthful man, one who had never done or achieved anything in his life. No need thinking about someone his own age, not when he had been promised a young woman, one who could give him a child and make him a father.

Bolt had picked up a few supplies and then headed out of town. He surveyed the terrain and made his decision to follow the road along the south side. While it was mostly grazing land or open country to the north, the land was mostly rolling hills and empty prairie. Off to the south were some rugged mountain ranges and only a sprinkle of diehard prospectors, small ranches or trappers. It stood to reason, anyone involved in kidnapping would choose their hideout where it was hard to access, yet easy to defend.

Riding about a hundred yards away from, but parallel to, the main road, Bolt searched the ground for fresh prints. He moved with care, dismounting to walk through sections of hard-packed earth or shale rock. His skill was not nearly equal to Scrapper Cobb, but he had done a lot of hunting. He knew a little about reading tracks.

It was early September, so the air had a bite to it in early morning or in the evening. When the sun went down the temperature dropped into the fifties or below. As there was a slight breeze blowing from the south, and the sky was clear, the weather was comfortable without a jacket for the painstaking search.

The sun was peeking in and out between some high, drifting clouds by the time he reached the small stream. It was the only crossing between Lost Bend and the way station that had water year around. Almost every other ditch or creek bed was dry by this time of year.

Standing at the edge of the brook, he allowed his horse to drink and took a long look around. To his surprise, he spotted two riders – both well off the main trail – obviously searching the ground. He loosened the cinch on his mount (the horse that had belonged to the dead bandit) and waited for Cobb and Deek to reach the diminutive waterway. Although less than a half-mile off, it took them thirty minutes before they arrived to join him.

'What say, Bolterfeld?' Cobb greeted him when they arrived.

The man looked as if he had been plucked from duty as an army scout – long, shaggy hair, bushy mustache, and a short beard that showed a lot of gray hair. His clothes were buckskins, including his jacket, with lace-up moccasin boots that nearly reached his knees. He sported a large skinning-knife on one hip and a Remington Army revolver on the other. Strapped to his horse was his trusty .50 Caliber Sharps hunting rifle.

'Cobb, you're a sight to behold,' Bolt told him. 'I didn't think you'd be here until well after dark.'

'Deek here found me whilst I was in camp. We started our hunt at the station and found something right interesting.'

'What's that?'

'Someone was up on a hill watching you folks. Crossed his trail on my first circle at the way station. I found where he was sittin' and it appears a couple other riders come to visit him. They rode off toward the hills, but he took a sharp angle to get ahead of the lady.'

Bolt shook his head. 'I'm slipping, Cobb. I didn't see any sign of being followed.'

'He wouldn't have needed to follow you,' Cobb said. 'He knew where you were going. We've been tracking him and it appears he headed to the creek at a fast pace. I'm betting the guy grabbed your missing gal right here.'

Leaving Deek with the horses, Cobb led the way

63

over to the main trail crossing. It took only a few minutes to locate the spot where the two horses had come together.

'Yep,' Cobb announced. 'Here's where they took to the water. I 'spect that there 'napper intended to throw off any pursuit by riding the creek.'

'I've been watching the south side all the way from town. Hasn't been any recent tracks, but I pretty much stayed within a few hundred yards of the trail.'

'No matter,' Cobb said. 'We'll start from here – you on one side and me on the other. I recall you're a fair tracker.'

'Anything I find, I'll get your opinion on it before we take off on a wild-goose chase.'

'Never chased any wild geese. They leave webbed prints on the ground?'

'No.' Bolt remained serious. 'You have to follow their flight pattern in the sky. Takes a heap of learning to follow that.'

Cobb chuckled. 'Good thing we ain't tracking geese. You take the east side of the bank and I'll take the west. Don't walk past nuthen you can't identify.'

Bolt looked off into the distance. 'It's maybe three miles until this stream hits the river. Looks like mostly rugged terrain ahead of us.'

'Yep. I reckon we'll find where they left the water long before the river. Once into the hard country beyond the rise, there's steep-walled canyons and mountains even goats don't try to cross. We don't want to end up trapped back there. Be a great place for an ambush.'

'Let's get to it. The sun won't last more than a few hours.'

CHAPTER SIX

Sirus Proctor, standing at the rear door, was surprised to see Tug Mackintosh and some men ride up to his luxury railroad car. His personal guard followed his orders. He allowed Big Mack to enter, but the five men with him were required to stay outside. Sirus took a seat behind his desk and waited.

Mack marched up to him and planted himself like a large oak tree, hands on his hips and an icy glare in his eyes.

Proctor rose politely and extended his hand in friendship. 'Mack,' he said easily. 'Been a long time.'

'Tell me to my face,' Mack demanded firmly. 'Tell me you have nothing to do with this.'

'I'm sorry.' Proctor displayed complete innocence. 'Whatever are you talking about?'

'The kidnapping of Ariette Ekhard,' Mack clarified. 'And the condition that I stop laying track until the ransom is paid.'

Proctor was appalled. 'Miss Ekhard? You mean Brock's daughter? She's been kidnapped?' He threw up his hands. 'My son told me about the attack on the stage, but he said your man, Bolterfeld, arrived to save her.'

Mack struggled with the next words. 'She run off during the night, told the stationer's kid she wanted to send a telegraph message to her father. Next thing, I'm getting a ransom demand.'

Proctor moved around his desk and stepped over to his liquor cabinet. He took out a bottle and two glasses.

'Instead of accusing me, Mack,' he said calmly, 'Try telling me what is going on. I don't have a clue as to why you think I would be behind something like this.'

Mack explained about the demand to stop laying track. He ended with, 'And, if this is a simple ransom, I can see no reason why the craven cowards would demand I stop going forward with rail.'

'Well,' Proctor countered, 'I think it's obvious.' Seeing Mack's increased glare, he explained. 'Whoever grabbed Brock's daughter must know you are in a race with me to reach the pass first. Forcing you to shut down your operation until the ransom is paid sounds like an extra measure of incentive. They know you must pay up or lose the race.'

Mack grudgingly admitted the logic made sense. 'But who could have known she was coming and what stage she was on?'

'Hard to say.'

'What about the outlaw who was killed? He sometimes worked for you.'

'Me?'

'Jack Rutledge, the guy with a harelip.'

Proctor harrumphed. 'Rutledge was a thief. My son caught him stealing several kegs of beer and a case of my expensive brandy. He was lucky that I only fired him. If there had been any law nearby, I'd have had him thrown in jail.'

'How long ago was this?'

Proctor didn't answer the question, but walked back to his desk. He opened a ledger and thumbed through several pages.

'Here it is,' he announced. 'Terminated the first week of July. He hasn't worked for me in two months.'

'But how would he know about the girl?'

'Jack had some unsavory pals, one of whom was a telegrapher during the war. He could have learned about the girl's travel plans, or some of his friends might have heard it from your men, or even someone at the railroad or express office.'

Mack took a sip of his drink and pondered a few moments. He knew Procter could lie like a politician. But he had never considered him low enough to stoop to something like kidnapping.

'If you need men to help with a search…?' Proctor offered.

'No, I've got capable men on that. We'll find the kidnappers; you can bank on that.'

Proctor emptied his glass and set it down. 'Mack,

I will do whatever I can to help, but you can't expect me to shut down my crews. You are much closer to the pass than I am.'

'A week would change that,' Mack said. 'If my rail-roaders are idle for a full week, I'll be the one forced to go around the mountain range.'

'I've already got my surveyors staking out the alternative route for us,' Proctor said. 'I'm realistic about my chances. I don't expect to reach the pass ahead of you.'

'I suppose you'll take your time and ignore this opportunity?'

Proctor laughed. 'Mack, we are competitors, and there is a lot of money at stake. I'm not above taking advantage of the situation.'

'Meaning?'

'I've already put a new work schedule in place.' He held up his hands in a calming gesture. 'Not because of this kidnapping. It was already in the works, and it's because I want to beat the winter weather. If there is an early blizzard, we could be stuck for weeks trying to finish the line.'

Mack knew there were many more accidents at night, plus the workers accomplished less when working by lanterns. However, Wyoming was notorious for ground blizzards and cold weather. He was only six weeks away from completion, so he didn't face the same concern. However, if he was forced to go around the mountains, the track would require an extra five or six weeks. That would land him in the middle of the winter weather.

'If you learn anything I ought to know,' he said to Proctor, 'I'd appreciate you letting me know.'

'Certainly, my friend,' the man replied. 'While we are rivals, we are not enemies. And the offer stands: anything I can do to help.' He grinned. 'Short of shutting down my own crews.'

Mack thanked him for the courtesy and drink, then went out to his waiting men. As he rode away from Proctor's car he worried that a loss of five or six days would be too long. He would pay the ransom as soon as the kidnappers made contact . . . anything to get Ariette back and resume building the railroad.

'Thinks he's pretty smart,' Cobb remarked to Deek and Bolt. 'Left the water where this smaller ditch spills into the creek.' He gestured to a narrow wash that had eroded a foot deep and a couple feet across. It derived from a shallow between three different hills, not enough to form a pool, but running water sought the least resistance and had created a small ditch to the stream.

Bolt had been riding on the opposite side of the stream. He crossed on his horse and rode to where Cobb was studying the ground.

'You got him?'

'Scrapes are fresh, not more than a few hours old. I'd wager he picked this spot because he could find it in the dark. He assumed the gravel along the bottom would be packed hard enough to not leave any prints.'

'Not a professional then,' Deek suggested.

'He's like a good many men – knows just enough to think he's smart. We've got him now. The second horse looks to have new irons.' He looked up at Bolt. 'You told Deek your steed had been shod recently.'

'That's right, only a couple of weeks back.'

Cobb remained on foot and began to follow the faint markings. Just before they reached the hollowed point where water would collect after a rain, he stopped.

'Here we go,' he said, inspecting the ground carefully. 'He took the horses over this patch or rock and headed toward that notch.'

Bolt looked at the small gorge, nestled between two hillocks. There was adequate ground cover, consisting of bunches of wild grass, some scattered sagebrush and a few scraggly patches of thistle. Taking a moment to study the ground, he grunted.

'I might have missed it, Cobb. Glad you are here.'

'There's a rundown ranch of sorts off that-away. I recollect riding past it when I was hunting fresh meat one time. Place didn't look like much, but I recall there was a corral with a couple horses.'

Bolt looked off toward where Lost Bend was located. 'It could be the Voight ranch. I remember someone in town mentioning they had a place out in the sticks.'

'If that outlaw family is mixed up in this, we'll have our hands full,' Deek directed his words at Bolt. 'Didn't you tell me the old man and his boys

71

lived out here?'

'Yes, but it wasn't the Voight bunch who hit the stage. We would have recognized them. Plus, as far as I know, the harelip who was killed didn't run with them.'

'We'll have to stay on the tracks,' Cobb suggested. 'It's possible this jasper was trying to make a false trail and throw us off his scent.'

'Right,' Bolt agreed. 'Stick with the kidnapper and see where he ends up.'

Ariette had long since eaten the crust of bread and drunk the flask of water, when she heard someone approach the door. It was dusk, so her tiny cubicle was quite dark. She had kept the blindfold handy, prepared for the visit.

'Slip the cloth over your eyes.' The voice was different from the captors she had heard or the man who had grabbed her at the creek crossing. He sounded more educated. 'Remember what you were told about being able to identify one of us.'

Ariette did as she was told and stated: 'I'm ready.'

The bottom of the door slid against the ground and she kept her head lowered. It allowed her to peer under the bottom of the blindfold and see the man's feet. Even though the sun had gone down, she had been in total blackness for most of the day. She was able to see that he wore expensive boots, with tiny silver medallions on the tips of the toes.

'Could I have a little more water?' she asked timidly. 'I would like to wash my hands and face.'

'Maybe in the morning,' he allowed. 'No one is making a second trip out here tonight.'

'Tomorrow would be fine.' She was again meek and gracious.

'Not exactly the treatment you're used to,' he jeered. 'No servants around to do your bidding.'

'I'm not complaining,' Ariette said softly. 'For kidnappers, you've been very considerate.'

She couldn't see his face, but she knew most men responded favorably to a woman's voice – if she chose the right inflection. He set down her food and drink without a word, then returned outside and closed the door.

As soon as the lock was shoved into place, Ariette removed the cloth from her eyes and moved to the wooden stool. She found a pan of stew and a tin cup full of water. The visitor had taken the empty plate and small water jug with him; she had no eating utensils.

With only the two dirty blankets, Ariette had to rely on what was at hand. She wished she had thought to stick a handkerchief in her jacket before leaving her belongings at the way station. Dejected at her limited options, she lifted her riding skirt and managed to tear a strip of cloth from the lining. She would use it as her cleaning cloth . . . and to wipe her fingers.

Gritting her teeth, she began to pick out the bits of meat and potatoes from the stew. She had thought the Indian woman's dish lacking flavor, but it had been delicious compared to this mess. The portion was meager and tasteless, but Ariette was hungry. She quickly consumed every bite. She wished she had kept back a bit of bread to sop up the gravy. Instead, she was forced to lap it up like a dog.

'If Amanda could only see me now.' She laughed without humor to herself. 'She would take a broom to this band of abductors and sweep them right into a jail cell.'

'Bet your gal is in that shed,' Cobb opined. 'See? That one took her food for the night, and brought back the empty dishes.'

The three of them had donned their jackets and were lying on their stomachs, a good hundred yards away, on the crest of a gentle slope. The ranch lay in a small valley, with a knoll some distance beyond the house and a range of mountains off to either side. There was no approach to the yard or buildings that wasn't pretty much out in the open. As for the ranch house, it was sizable, probably five or six rooms, but the outside was in dire need of repair. To the far side, the pole corral had seen better days, but penned within were close to a dozen horses.

'Wish I had my field glasses,' Bolt said. 'I can't make out anyone clearly from this distance.'

'The coyote is mostly a blur to my sorry eyes,' Cobb complained.

'Looks as if that fellow is leaving,' Deek observed. 'Must have just stopped by to see and feed the prisoner.'

As they watched the man handed the pan and cup to another man on the porch. They exchanged a few words and then he mounted up and rode out of the yard. His direction was across the mouth of the nearby box canyon.

'Either going to town or to Proctor's line,' Cobb said. 'Maybe even to our own railroad. Could be a spy.'

'How many men do you think are down there?' Deek asked. 'Sure hope it ain't one for every mount left in that corral.'

'I've counted five different men so far, other than the rider who just left.' Bolt said. 'Two of the gang look like the Voight brothers Deek and I faced in town. A second pair looked similar – might be related. The other one looks like one of the guys who hit the stagecoach.'

'A lot of shadows have gone by the main window,' Cobb warned. 'We could be up against ten guns or more.'

'Too many for the three of us,' Deek said. 'How about we get a posse, or round up fifty or so men from the railroad?'

'They might move the girl come morning,' Bolt said. 'At the very least, they will be keeping watch. Don't want to risk her life if we can help it.' Even as he spoke, a man came out of the house with a big rifle in the crook of his arm. He walked to the corral and picked up a bridle.

'Yep,' Cobb said. 'There goes the night guard. He'll probably find a place up on high ground and spend the night keeping watch.'

The trio remained flat on the ground so as to not put a silhouette against the skyline. The man saddled a horse from the corral. Soon as he was aboard, he took a short circle around the outbuildings. He appeared to inspect the nearby area before he angled up to a hillock beyond the ranch house that overlooked the valley. From that point, he could see everything below and survey the surroundings for nearly a mile in any direction.

'So much for us being able to take him out quietly,' Cobb lamented. 'If he's a good shot, he could nail all three of us from that knoll before we reached the girl.'

Deek was also disheartened. 'Supposing we get her? The three of us sure can't take on a gang that size.'

'Not many fighting men in Lost Bend,' Bolt stated. 'To get any help, we'd have to recruit a gang from our railroaders. That would take too long.'

'Looks like we handle it ourselves,' Cobb concluded. 'Who's got a plan?'

'You said it yourself, Bolt,' Deek added. 'There's no help at Lost Bend. If we grab the girl, our only chance would be to head for the railroad.'

'It's twenty miles closer to ride for Proctor's end-of-tracks rather than our own camp,' Bolt reasoned. 'We could make that in a day.'

'On fresh horses, maybe,' Cobb said. 'With the corral on the other side of the yard, we can't trade out our mounts, let alone grab a horse for the lady.'

Bolt studied the terrain for a time. It was growing ever darker, but the clouds had dissipated overhead and the moon would be bright within a short while. The time to move was during full darkness.

'You're right about the corral, it's completely out in the open,' he said. 'But I see a pretty good route to the shed. If they don't put a guard on her door, I might be able to slip down there and get the girl out.'

'Then what?' Deek asked. 'There's already a glow of light where the moon is about to show its face. No way the two of you can make it all the way back without being seen.'

'Not if that sentry is alert,' Bolt admitted. 'Miss Ekhard has no training when it comes to stealth. But we might be able to reach the edge of where the sagebrush spills into the valley.' He gestured at the open ground furthermost from the house and shed, at the opposite side of the valley from the corral. 'If you two stayed in the shadows and got our horses fairly close, we might get mounted before the guard spotted us. Once moving, we would be a quarter-mile away. Even if he saw us, it's doubtful he could hit a target in the dark from that distance.'

'Less'n he's an ex-buffalo hunter,' Cobb dissented. 'Back before my eyes gave out for long-distance, I could have knocked all four of us from horseback from atop that hill he's on.'

'We could hold off until early hours of the morning,' Dee intimated. 'The guard might doze off.'

'The moon would be full and bright by then,' Bolt replied to that option. 'I don't want to give the man a better shot than necessary. Besides, it would shorten the amount of time we have to escape during the night.'

'I agree,' Cobb said. 'We've got maybe thirty minutes before the moon is shining down on us. We take our chances with the darkness.'

The three men inched slowly back from the crest of the hill until they were out of sight. Once Cobb and Deek were leading the horses to the low side of the slope, Bolt began to move himself.

CHAPTER SEVEN

Staying close against the hill was his best cover, but Bolt was forced to move at a snail's pace. Motion at night was easy to spot for a trained sentry. Anyone who had ever stood guard at night learned to memorize every bush, tree or rock formation, all before the sun went down. Then he would review it as darkness fell, because night distorted what the mind remembered from daylight. Once the guard was satisfied he knew each and every landmark, he would begin the conscientious routine of scanning. That meant moving your focus perpetually, enough to keep from seeing false movement: stare at a distant object long enough and it would appear to move. By allowing his gaze to traverse the terrain constantly, even the slightest movement would catch his eye.

As Bolt approached the base of the incline, he eased down on his hands and knees. Reaching an open area, he flattened out on his stomach and crawled, literally inch-by-inch until he reached the yard area.

It was a fairly cool night, but sweat beaded his brow. This was one time when he knew the myth of *not hearing the shot that killed you* would be true. Get shot from twenty feet away and the sound would be in a man's ears at the same time as the bullet. But from a couple hundred yards? There would be an almost half-second delay between getting hit and the echo of the gun blast.

Stop fretting about what you wouldn't be alive to worry about later, he scolded himself.

Working diligently, practically slithering like a snake, Bolt finally reached a place low enough to put the ranch house between him and the sentry. Using the building for cover, he padded silently up to within a few feet of the structure. There was a single window on each side of the house, but all of them were presently closed to keep out the evening chill. He could hear men's voices from within, but the conversation was subdued, as if some of them had bedded down for the night.

Bolt moved into the shadow of the building. Dangerous, because he was exposed to both the house – should anyone look out the window or step out for a smoke – and to the sentry on the hill. However, the guard would be unlikely to be watching for movement near the house, not with several men possibly coming and going until they all bedded down for the night. If Bolt could reach the shed undetected, their plan had a chance.

Taking a deep breath, he listened to the sounds emanating from within the house. He didn't detect anyone moving toward the door, and there was little reason for someone to be looking out the window. At least one lamp burned inside, but curtains covered the panes – if burlap sacks could be considered curtains. Releasing the pent-up air from his lungs slowly, Bolt walked boldly, and without haste, from the house to the shed. There was a prickling sensation down the back of his neck, as he expected a yell of alarm or the explosion of gunfire at any moment.

A few steps more brought him to the shed door. It was secured with a large 'L'-shaped bolt that fit into a hole in the frame. Bolt leaned in close against the door, masking his shadow with the darkness of the building.

'Miss Ekhard?' he whispered. 'Are you in there?'

There came a sudden scrambling noise from movement. A moment later an excited, yet carefully muted voice queried:

'Who's that? Who's out there?'

'It's Bolt. I'm here to get you out.'

'Careful,' she warned in a hushed voice. 'The door squeaks and drags on the ground.'

He took hold of the short leg of the deadbolt and slowly worked it back and forth, pulling it ever so gently. Once he had eased the rod free of the frame, he began to ease open the door. Ariette was right. The hinges were rusted and warped with age. Moving it even an inch caused a grating sound that seemed as loud as a ringing church bell. He tried lifting at the same time, but it was an incredibly slow process. It was pull and stop ... listen for a few moments, then repeat the process.

Ariette began to squeeze through as soon as there was room, sucking in her breath and holding her skirt tight to her hips. Once she was out Bolt put an arm around her and pinned her tight against the building.

'There's a guard up on a hill keeping watch,' he whispered next to her ear. 'Stay as close to the shed as you can. The horses are just about in position.'

'How did you ever find me?' she asked softly.

'Luck,' he replied. 'And we're going to need a lot more of it to get you to safety.'

'It can't be more than a few miles to town,' she said.

'The people in town aren't fond of this family, but they won't stand up to them either. I counted six or seven men in the place.'

'I lost count of voices,' she admitted. 'And they've been careful not to speak around me. I've not seen a single man's face.'

Bolt and the girl rounded the corner of the shed. It put them in a safer place if someone stepped out of the house. Bolt's eyes were adjusted to the black of night, and he saw Cobb and Deek as they reached the hollow beyond the brush-strewn field.

'This is it,' he warned the girl. 'If we walk very slow the sentry might not see us. However, we would be easy targets for him to hit. If we race for the horses it will make shooting more difficult, but the guard will have time to fire several shots. Either way, the first shot will bring men spilling out of the main ranch house.'

'What do you suggest?'

'We'll split the difference and walk normally. The guard might think it's a couple of the men checking the grounds. If he holds off until we reach the horses we'll have a chance to escape before the whole bunch is on our tail.'

'My riding skirt will give me away.'

Bolt knew she was right. He began to figure a way to hide her garb when she said, 'Wait! I've got an idea.'

Cautious of her movements, Ariette moved back around to the shed door and entered the shack. Bolt followed along and saw she had recovered a short length of rope.

'We can tie the split skirt to either side. It will still look a little bulky, but it won't look so much like a woman's dress.'

Even as she began to twist and pull half the skirt around one leg, Bolt cut the cord in two. He quickly tied off each side just above the knee, and it did give the appearance of bulky trousers. Soon as the cloth was bound in place, they returned out the door. To hide their escape, Bolt took a few precious seconds to close and secure the latch. If no one spotted them, they might not miss the girl until breakfast.

As they began to inch around the structure the girl grabbed his wrist. 'It's getting lighter!' she gasped.

'Moon is coming out,' Bolt said tightly. 'For a

sharp-eyed sentry, it will be like daylight. We've got to move. Now!'

They began the walk toward the open end of the yard. The tract of land where the horses were waiting looked a mile away. And with the moon's glow added to illuminate the world, Deek and Cobb had to remain next to the hill. If they broke cover the guard would surely see them.

Something hissed past their heads and kicked up dust not five feet in front of them. It was followed an instant later by the blast of a large-caliber rifle.

Bolt knew it was a warning shot to stop them. It would also rouse everyone in the house. They were out of luck and out of time.

'Run!' he shouted.

Cobb and Deek each mounted a horse as Bolt and the girl fled on foot. Deek was leading Bolt's horse and Cobb was yelling that they would could pick them up as they rode past.

'Lift your left arm and grab hold of the first rider,' Bolt shouted at Ariette.

The three horses and two riders broke into the open at a run. Cobb bore down on the girl and he caught hold of her. It was a struggle, but he dragged her off her feet and up until she could maneuver behind him.

Deek was holding out the reins to Bolt's horse when he suddenly folded over the saddle. As another gunshot echoed in the night, Deek lost hold of the third mount. It spooked and veered away. Before Bolt could make a grab for it, the animal headed for the corral beyond the ranch house – likely the last place it had been fed and watered before the attack on the stage.

Bolt's only option was to catch hold of Deek's saddle and swing up behind him. He managed the feat as a third shot rang out. This time Bolt felt the sting of a bullet as it grazed the flesh above his knee.

The horse stumbled but righted itself. It kept running after Cobb's mount and they were quickly over a rise and out of range. Trouble was, the quickest route away from the shooter had been to head toward the box canyon, which was two or three miles deep.

Bolt urged more speed, but the game little mount had obviously been hit. It gave what it could, but didn't last but a short way. It managed to get over a second rise, before it began to slow down.

Bolt shouted at Cobb as his steed had run itself to the point of collapse. Even as the gallant little pony staggered to a stop, Bolt wrapped his arms around Deek and pulled him to the ground. The horse sank to its knees, then lay down on his side. Bolt laid Deek on the ground and paused long enough to stroke the gelding's neck. After a few ragged breaths, the animal lay still. A shot to end its misery was not needed.

'S-sorry,' Deek wheezed, lifting his head and grimacing with pain. 'Looks like I made a mess of the escape.'

'Yeah,' Bolt agreed. 'Real careless of both you and your horse to let yourselves be shot like that.'

Bolt was examining his friend's injury as Cobb and the girl returned. Cobb got down and watched over Bolt's shoulder. After folding a piece of cloth against the wound in Deek's side, the two of them wrapped a strip of cloth around Deek's middle to hold the bandage in place and stop the bleeding.

'Doesn't look too bad,' Cobb observed. 'Bullet went in and out pretty clean. If it didn't tear up his vitals along its path, he should pull through.'

'Not without medical treatment,' Bolt replied. 'We have to get him to town. The doctor there is the one who wrote to him about his sister's abuse.'

'Boy, howdy!' Cobb declared. 'How are we going to do that?'

Bolt stood up and looked around. 'The Voight gang will be saddling their horses by this time. It's still too dark to track, but they might make a sweep of the area.' He thought for a moment. 'If it was me, I would send a couple men to cut us off from town.'

Cobb snorted. 'You said they ain't feared of no one in town. They might expect us to head to genuine safety – the end-of-tracks.'

'You're right,' Bolt agreed. 'The real danger to them is if we get fifty men from the railroad and hunt them down like the murdering kidnappers they are.'

'So, what's your idea?' Cobb asked. 'We've got one horse for a wounded man, a city-bred gal, and the two of us.'

'One of us will have to take Deek to town. That means avoiding the men sent to intercept anyone going that direction or toward the railroad.'

'You take the horse. I can be a ghost in the wild,' Cobb bragged. 'I've escaped more bloodthirsty Injuns than you've ever set eyes on. Even on foot, them boys won't catch me.'

'But with your poor eyesight you can't see to shoot at anything more than a few yards away,' Bolt reminded him. 'With the girl in tow, we can't let that bunch get within shooting distance.'

Cobb squawked: 'I see where this is going. I'm to nursemaid Deek to town, then get word to Big Mack that you and his bride are playing cat and mouse with a dozen guns out in the hills.'

'We'll head for Proctor's camp. His line is west of here. I doubt it's more than fifteen or twenty miles away.'

'But this here is a dead-end canyon, Bolt. You get into it fur enough and a horse can't climb out. Then, as you get deeper in, the walls keep growing higher and steeper every step of the way. How you going to climb out of something like that with a society-raised filly in tow?'

'We'll do it because we don't have a choice. How many rounds do you have for your Sharps rifle?'

'Thirty. I never carry less than that.'

'And its range?'

'Billy Dixon used one just like mine at the second battle of Adobe Wells last June. Newspaper story said he kilt an Injun at just over fifteen hundred yards.'

'That should give us a big advantage. What are

your sights set for?'

'Five hundred yards ... cause I can't see no further than that on the best of days.'

Bolt helped Ariette down and then took the buffalo gun and ammunition from Cobb. The ex-scout paused to warn him:

'You did take notice of how that shooter put a slug through Deek and killed your mount? He was at two or three hundred yards and shooting in the dark.'

'If he follows us I'll take him out first,' Bolt promised.

The two of them loaded Deek on the horse and Cobb climbed up behind him. After wishing them luck Bolt watched the two of them angle off in the direction of Lost Bend.

'Can they make it?' Ariette asked. 'I mean, you said the kidnappers would be watching.'

'Cobb will avoid any riders,' Bolt said with confidence. 'He knows every trick there is about tracking or getting through hostile territory undetected. And, it's like he said, the Voight family won't expect any of us to head for town. They have cowed the few townsmen ever since they came to this part of the country.'

'What about us?'

Bolt went over to the dead horse and removed the saddle-bags, bedroll and canteen. He then used the rawhide straps from the saddle to make a sling for the long gun. With his gunbelt full of ammo for his revolver, he tied the sack of .50-.90 cartridges to his belt. While he was doing that, Ariette removed the rope from each leg so her riding-skirt would not be so cumbersome to walk in.

'You carry the canteen and bedroll; I'll carry the saddle-bags.' He surveyed the area and saw that the canyon's walls had already begun to rise at either side. They would stay close to the northern wall and find a place to make their first stand. After that, it would be a matter of ambush, retreat, elude, and ambush again. The only thing in his favor was the hunting party would want to take the girl alive. Unfortunately, he couldn't count on that remaining so . . . not after his first defensive stand.

Mortimer was there to meet Eagle-eye as soon as he arrived in the yard. They had already looked inside the shed and discovered the girl was gone. The others were all saddling their horses.

'What happened?' he asked the man. 'I thought you were the pride of the Southern Confederacy – best marksman and sharpest eyes in the whole damn army!'

As was his habit, Eagle-eye ignored the criticism. He didn't work for Voight.

'There were three men in the rescue party,' he said. 'I hit one of them pretty good and he lost one of their horses.' He tipped his head toward town. 'Must have been Jack's mount because it headed for the corral.'

'We ain't interested in a single horse!'

'You should be,' Eagle-eye advised him. 'By the

time the girl and third man were aboard, I put a slug into a second horse and might have also nicked the rider. They skedaddled over the rise, heading for the canyon. I doubt they'll get far before that second mount is down.'

Mortimer paused, his disgust reversed to amazement. 'You did that much damage from atop the south hill, with only three shots?'

'I wasted my first shot trying to stop them. Once they took off running, I had no trouble deciding which one was the girl, so I cut down one of the men and his horse.'

Ethan and Wily came over to hear the last of the report. Ethan looked to his brother for their orders. Wily waited patiently, not saying a word.

'They could turn and head for town,' Eagle-eye suggested. 'They might think it offers a safe haven.'

'Not if any of the three were ever around town for more than a few hours,' Mortimer informed him. 'We run roughshod over the whole valley. Everyone knows not to mess with us.'

'Then their safest bet is the end-of-tracks,' Ethan guessed. 'We'll have to head them off.'

'One horse for the four of them,' Eagle-eye outlined, 'and one man badly injured or dead. They must have been tracking Handy all day to get here, meaning their lone animal is about spent.'

'Eagle-eye, you take Ethan's two boys and cut them off from the railroad. The rest of us will get on their tracks and run them to ground.'

'We'll stop them, should they make for the rail-road,' Eagle-eye promised. 'Wily, you and Handy track for these boys.'

'Whatever you say, pard,' Wily replied.

Ethan remained with his older brother as Eagle-eye hurried off to pick up Abe and Butcher. Ethan didn't hide his vexation.

'This ain't good, Mortimer. Suppose the gal gets away?'

'Eagle-eye says he hit one of the three men, and maybe a second. They only have one horse and the girl don't know squat about us. If they try to ride double with her, we'll have them an hour after sunup.'

'So we stick to the plan as if she is still tucked away in the storage shed?'

'Exactly. Nothing has changed as far as Mackintosh is concerned. We'll kill them three bloodhounds that found us and no one will be the wiser.'

'Works fine for us,' Wily interjected. 'Eagle-eye will sure enough cut anyone off before they can reach the railroad. He's the best shot and tracker in these parts.'

'He proved he could shoot,' Ethan admitted.

Mortimer swore and clenched his fists. 'I got to wonder how the devil they found us so quick? One of them fellas must be an extraordinary tracker.'

'Yep.' Ethan grinned. 'Reckon he's good enough that he just tracked himself to his own death!'

'Let's get saddled up. We'll start out slow, spread

wide, and head up the canyon. We'll make sure no one slips past us in the dark. Come full light, we'll pick up their tracks. Quick as we figure where they went, we'll hunt them down easy enough.'

'I hear you,' Ethan said back.

'I'll go ahead and take the ransom demand to town,' Wily said. 'Unless you think this might change things?'

'No, go ahead,' Mortimer replied. 'You can catch up with us in the morning.'

Wily left to get his horse and Mortimer didn't speak again, staring out into the night. Everything had been going without a hitch. The ransom note would still arrive, the timetable was in place, and they only needed to set up an exchange point. But now they would have to work a lot harder for their big payday. Whoever had grabbed the girl must have been good. How else could they have found her so quick? It was imperative that they catch or kill all three men and get the girl back. Regrettably, it stood to reason the men who grabbed the girl knew their identities . . . his family's at least.

Ducking his head, he cursed the trio of men who had found their hideout. The girl wasn't supposed to learn who had kidnapped her. Pondering along those lines, he thought of Eagle-eye. The man had proved he could hit targets that were a long way off, with only the moonlight to see by. They would choose the right place for the exchange, one where they could keep watch on everything from a distance. Once they had their money, Eagle-eye could take out the girl. It was cold-blooded and ruthless, but the alternative was to never be safe again.

CHAPTER EIGHT

Bolt moved with as much speed as the girl could manage. Being raised a proper young lady, she had not done a lot of hiking and rock climbing. She was game in the respect of not complaining and did her best to keep up. Even when she was puffing and grunting from the hurried pace, she said not a word of protest.

After two hours of moving carefully they were well into the canyon. Bolt located a likely place and stopped for a breather. Ariette collapsed to the ground, utterly jaded. She lay on her back, arms out at her sides, her chest heaving with exertion.

It was about midnight, the moon was overhead, and Bolt took time to inspect the Sharps rifle. The barrel looked clear and the chamber accepted the first of his thirty rounds. He lifted the weapon to his shoulder and took a practice aim, getting the feel of the gun and its weight. His preference was his Winchester '73, but it had been on the horse Deek had lost when he couldn't hold its reins. Knowing how careful and efficient Cobb was about his weapons, he knew the Sharps would be ready to fire. He propped the rifle against a rock and sat down a couple feet from Ariette.

The girl was still laboring to catch her breath, so Bolt picked up the canteen and offered it to her.

'Just a sip or two,' he cautioned. 'We might find fresh water between here and the railroad and we might not. A lot of people become sick or die from drinking stagnant water.'

Ariette sat up and accepted the offered container. She took exactly two sips, handed it back, then she lay back down.

'Guess you haven't done a lot of mountain climbing, huh?'

A slight smile curled her lips upward. 'Don't find many hills in the city. I once shopped in a large clothing and mercantile store that was four stories high. I managed to climb their stairs once or twice.'

'We will have some hard climbing when we reach the end of this canyon. It's a couple of miles yet.'

'So we scale a solid rock wall and then waltz another ten or fifteen miles to the railroad. Ought to be a snap.'

'You're what is called a *gamer*, Miss Ekhard,' he complimented her. 'A good many refined ladies would be whining or complaining about facing such hardship. To this point, you've been up to the challenge.'

'I can be practical when the need arises, Mr Bolt.'

'Practical? As in agreeing to marry Big Mack, then

running away?'

Even in the dark, he saw shame flood her features. 'I lost my nerve,' she murmured. 'Saving the family fortune seems a noble cause, but marrying a man twice my age, a man I've never met. . . .' She didn't have to finish the sentence.

'On Mack's behalf, he is a nice guy – fair, caring, with a gentle disposition.'

'My father is all those things,' she argued. 'It doesn't mean I want to marry a duplicate of him.' She stared at Bolt with an odd expression. 'Do you know that I've never even been courted by a man like you?'

'Like me?'

'You know what I mean, a well-traveled man, one who has known danger and crossed unknown territory; a man who is confident because of his ability, not because his father controls a bank, business or railroad. Every suitor who was ever allowed to court me was fine-tailored, lettered, and an insufferable snob. Not one of them has ever stood on their own, taken up arms against bandits or Indians, or risked their lives to help someone else.'

'Risking your life is usually a foolish thing,' Bolt replied.

'You risked your life for Deek, a man you didn't even know.'

Bolt cleared his throat from embarrassment. 'Yes, but I had nothing to lose. I'm not responsible for anything or anyone. If I'd have had a wife and children, I would not have been so quick to put my life on the line.'

'You miss my point, Mr Bolt,' she said. 'It is the fact you were *willing* to help a man you didn't know, to put his life ahead of your own safety – that's what I'm talking about. The men I've associated with were priggish, pampered and self-absorbed. They would never risk their life and limb to help someone else, not even a friend or relative.'

'I also bring to the table a single-minded temperament, and I've an unabiding dislike for big-talkers or people who look down on someone because they are poor or don't share the same values,' he responded. 'I'm not a preaching sort, but I do think respect for others and a firm morality is necessary for man to rise above the animals.'

'I find no fault with your stance,' Ariette remarked. 'Plus, you have twice saved me from harm. I will never forget that.'

'I was only doing my job.'

'No one would have thought less of you for sending for help tonight, rather than rescuing me on your own.'

'Yes, and it might turn out to have been a mistake. If you're caught. . . .'

'I won't blame you one tiny bit.' She cut his sentence short. 'Regardless of whether we get away or are both killed, I'm the one responsible for being in this predicament and I'm grateful to you for the rescue.'

Not knowing how to respond to her statement, Bolt turned to the desperate situation at hand.

'Get some sleep,' he proposed. 'An hour or so before first light, we'll head deeper into the canyon. I want to be in position when those varmints come after us.'

'No one can follow in this total darkness,' Ariette countered. 'You should get some rest, too.'

'I'll maybe close my eyes for a few minutes.'

'You can't be comfortable laying your head against a rock. I'll spread out the poncho for a ground sheet and we can share the blanket. It will keep us both warmer during the chill of the night.'

Bolt was stunned at the offer. 'I couldn't do that.'

'Are you afraid of me?'

'You? No.' He felt a warmth rise up his throat. 'It's just . . . well, it wouldn't be proper.'

She laughed derisively. 'Mr Bolt, we're running for our lives and will likely die tomorrow. Where's the harm in sharing a blanket? It's not like we're sharing a bed. Wearing all of our clothes, you won't even touch my bare skin.'

Bare skin!

A shiver ran through Bolt, a nervous anticipation that was a mix of terror and elation. The notion of being so close to Ariette caused wild sensations, uncontrollable thoughts, and not a small measure of guilt. Never had he felt so strongly about a girl, and in such a short period of time. But this woman was promised to the man he worked for, a man he respected, a man who trusted him. He dared not allow his guard to drop for a single second, or he feared he would be swept away by an uncontrollable desire to possess her.

Ke-ripes, Bolt! he admonished himself. *Buck up and act like a man!* Upon review of that thought, he amended the notion. *No! Not an ordinary man! Make it a man with no interest in this young lady, a lady who is quite possibly the sweetest, prettiest, most wonderful girl you'll ever meet.*

Boldly, assuming a cool veneer he didn't feel, Bolt moved over next to the girl. She had already arranged the poncho for them to lie on. As he settled down at her side, she flipped the blanket so it would cover them both. Then she placed her head on her lightweight jacket, folded to make herself a pillow, and sighed contentedly.

'See?' she teased. 'Just like a couple of friends, out enjoying the moon and stars. Doesn't that beat placing your head on a dirty old rock and ending up with a stiff neck and back from trying to doze while sitting up?'

'Uh, yeah,' he managed, wondering why his collar felt so snug.

'When I was a little girl,' Ariette said. 'I remember my big sister taking me out on the balcony of our house. We would sit in a couple of lounging chairs and she would tell me stories about the different books she had read.'

'Stories without the work of reading . . . sounds like fun.'

'Sometimes we would also read together. A book that would take several days usually lasted us about two nights. My sister and I would stay up reading by candlelight until the wee hours of the morning. Made Father absolutely furious.

'She married?'

'Yes, and quite appropriately, her husband owns a fair-sized library.'

After a short silence Bolt remarked: 'Did you know cowpokes often use the stars to keep track of time when riding night herd.'

'No,' she admitted. 'But I did read that hundreds of years ago, seafaring Phoenicians taught other sailors how to use the Little Dipper constellation to navigate by night.'

'Never been on a real ship, although I traveled by riverboat one time.'

'So what is your actual name?' Ariette asked, changing the direction of the conversation. 'Mr Cobb calls you Bolterfeld, so Bolt is obviously the short version of that title.'

'Bolterfeld is my last name.'

'So what is the rest of your name. Are you ashamed of it?'

'It is mildly embarrassing.'

'I won't laugh,' she promised. 'Please, I would really like to know.'

After a short pause, he quietly confessed: 'Romeo Lester Bolterfeld – named after my mother's favorite literary character and her father. Pa was off on a job the month I was born and didn't have any input when it came to naming me.'

The girl was oddly silent. He cast a sidelong glance at her and saw she had put her hand over her mouth. It wasn't adequate – she started to laugh.

'You promised,' he reminded her.

'Oh, it's not the name . . .' with a giggle, 'I've known a couple other men named Lester.'

'Funny,' he said drily.

'Actually, I quite enjoyed the story of Romeo and Juliet.'

'Man and woman kill themselves? Not the kind of ending for me.'

'You think they should have stole away in the dead of night? Where would they have gone? How would they have lived?'

'Long as you've got a breath in your body, you have a chance. Suicide is the coward's way out.'

'So, will you rewrite our ending, my Romeo?'

'*Bolt* is my preferred name,' he reminded her. 'I never figured I would be able to live up to a first name like that and didn't relish being called Lester. Bolterfeld is a mouthful, so I always went by Bolt.'

Ariette yawned and Bolt knew they only had a couple hours before they had to start moving again. He would have loved to talk to the girl all night, but they both would need what rest they could get. The arduous task ahead would in all probability sap every bit of their strength.

'Try and get some sleep,' he told her softly. 'I'll wake you when we have to get started.'

She closed her eyes and there was a jaded dreaminess in her voice. 'Whatever you say, Bolt. I trust you will take care of me.'

Bolt attempted to blot out the fact he was lying

next to such a desirable woman. He closed his eyes and mentally pushed the active thoughts from his mind. Two or three hours' sleep and then it would be a long day ahead. There was a good chance, it would be the last day of his life.

The sun cast long shadows into the canyon as Handy walked around the area of the fallen horse. After a time he came over to Mortimer and Ethan.

'They split up,' he informed the two men. 'There's a little blood on the ground – likely the first man Eagle-eye shot. I'd guess he and one other rode the one remaining horse and they headed off towards the railroad.'

'Eagle-eye should cut them off,' Mortimer said with confidence. 'It's forty miles to Mackintosh's end of the rails.'

'What about the other two?' Ethan wanted to know.

'Their tracks show they are moving deeper into the canyon.'

'Maybe they don't know it's a box canyon?' Ethan said.

'The girl is on foot,' Handy announced. 'That means the two of them won't make very good time.'

'They've nowhere to go,' Mortimer remarked. 'That don't seem very smart.'

'Only option for them,' Handy mused. 'It's a lot of open country if they tried to reach town or head off toward Proctor's camp.'

'Then we've got them trapped.'

'I suppose a man could climb out somewhere along the way, but it will be hard for a woman. You seen the way the gal was dressed, and her shoes were not meant for scaling cliffs.'

'Let's get after them,' Ethan said. 'Soon as we get the gal back we only have to make sure that Eagle-eye did his job. That would put everything back to where we started.'

'Ransom note should be at the railroad sometime today. That means we only have to wait four more days to collect.'

Handy stared at the rough country ahead. Uneven canyon floor, with rocky slopes to either side. The rising walls had dips and ridges, lined with tangle-brush and towering precipices. Did the man think he actually had a chance to escape? He gave a shake of his head. 'Seems too easy.'

'You read the prints,' Mortimer countered. 'One man and the girl. We're only after one man. The girl sure ain't no sharpshooter.'

'It's the one man that troubles me,' Handy said. 'I told you about the joker who shot Jack. He was on the back of a running horse, close to a hundred yards away, and he cut Jack down before he could get away.'

'Lucky shot,' Ethan reckoned.

'His first bullet hit the stage's door, a few inches from Jack's head,' Handy argued. 'And that was a sight further away than when he kilt him.'

'So what's your point?'

'My point is, this could be the guy with the girl. If

103

it is, he's one hell of a shot!'

'There's six of us and only one of him,' Mortimer declared. 'He ain't gonna take us all on at one time.'

Wily Kolt came over to join them. He had returned from sticking the ransom letter under the door of the general store in town. His eyes were red from lack of sleep, but he had a determined look on his face.

'What's the hold-up, Handy?' he asked. 'The boss thinks we have the girl ready for the exchange. We've got to get her back.'

'Yeah, well the boss ain't here to risk his neck, is he,' Handy fired back. 'I've got a bad feeling about this fellow we're tracking. He must have a plan of some kind.'

'What plan?' Mortimer cried. 'Eagle-eye shot the extra horse, hit one of his men and downed this second animal. His plan was done in by Eagle-eye's keen shooting. He's on foot and running for his life.'

'We need to get after them,' Wily said. 'Let's not give him time to stop and think.'

'All right.' Handy succumbed to the pressure. 'Keep the men spread out and ready to shoot. If our prey opens up on us we'll have to pepper him with lead before he can get the range and hit any of us.'

'I'll take my two sons and cover the left side. Ethan can stick with you two and cover the right. That way, he won't have any of us bunched up,' said Mortimer.

As one, all of them moved to get mounted. Handy would try and track from the back of his horse, but he figured the two fugitives would soon move into the rocks for cover. Then he would have to follow on foot. The girl would slow the pair down, and that was both good and bad. The good part: he would catch them before the day was done; the bad part: when he did, the man was likely to turn and fight. It was entirely possible this was the very same man who had killed Jack, and he hated the idea of being one of his targets.

Mack was dining with Mrs Peterson (he hated eating alone, so she always cooked for the two of them), when Scrappy Cobb entered the car. His shoulders were sagging and his hair was damp and pasted to his scalp as he removed his floppy old hat.

'Brought you the ransom note,' he began. 'It arrived whilst I was with Deek, over at the doctor's place. I rousted out the store owner to get the letter and rode all night to get here.'

'What do you mean – Deek was at the doctor's?'

Cobb uttered an 'ahem' and added: 'I've got another bit of news.'

Mack gestured to a chair. 'Mrs Peterson,' he spoke to the woman, 'another plate and some coffee for Mr Cobb.'

Cobb sat down and explained the chain of events. When finished, he handed Mack the letter.

'So you rescued Ariette, but now Bolt is out there with her alone? Just the two of them?'

'Deek wanted to get back, but he'd lost quite a bit of blood. The doctor thinks he will pull through, but not if he don't get some rest.'

'I'm surprised the kidnappers allowed you to get to town.'

'I left a trail like we were headed here, then cut back and waited until I seen three riders heading that direction. They are probably still wondering where we went.'

'And you took the railroad route to get here, so they were off in the opposite direction and wouldn't cross yourr tracks.'

'That's it exactly.'

The lady returned with a plate, utensils and a cup of coffee. Cobb sipped a couple swallows of the coffee and then looked at Mack.

'Give me a couple hours to rest up and I'll lead some men to find and rescue Bolterfeld. He is going to try and reach Proctor's end of the line, being that it's a whole lot closer to where the canyon ends than to come our way.'

'Ariette has to keep up with Bolt, scale the wall of a canyon, then walk twenty miles to the railroad?'

Cobb heaved his shoulders in a shrug. 'Once we were down to one horse, with a wounded man, we didn't have a lot of options, Mack.'

He took a moment to study the ransom note. 'Twenty-five thousand dollars. And they will contact us as to the place and time.' Mack crumpled up the note. 'I would pay it tomorrow, if we could get Ariette and Bolt back right away. The girl's safety is paramount, but we also need to get back to work. Proctor has his men laying track around the clock. Every day we lose is a day closer to having him reach Breakneck Pass before we do.'

'We should know by tonight or early tomorrow if you have to pay anything at all,' Cobb said. 'Soon as I catch a couple hours' sack time, I'll be ready to go.'

'Three days is all I gave the railroaders off,' Mack said. 'The minute we know Ariette is safe, we'll put our work crews on twenty-four-hour shifts until we hit the pass. Once we are securely beyond that point, we can go back to regular shifts. The race will have been won.'

Cobb had begun eating. He paused between mouthfuls. 'Most of the roustabouts are fair hands with guns and horses. It'd save me some time if you could get a few men ready to ride. Shouldn't need more than a dozen or so. I'll lead them towards Proctor's line and then head for the canyon. We will continue on until we meet up with Bolterfeld.'

Mack could not hide his amazement. 'You really believe Bolt will make it that far? I mean, the three men who missed you will be on this side of the canyon, and you said there might be as many as six or eight more on Bolt's trail right now!'

'Of all people I know, I wouldn't expect you to be the one to doubt what that man can do. He's a smart feller and a durned good shot. Them boys after him is like a pack of rats trying to bring down a cougar.'

Mack smiled at Cobb's support. 'I admit, Bolt is

the most competent man I ever met. I'll have the roustabout foreman gather some armed men and horses.'

Cobb picked up a slice of toast and rose from the table. 'Have them wake me in two hours and we'll get on our way.'

'You sure you only need two hours? You might be searching for Bolt all night.'

'Just like back fighting Injuns. I can catch up on my sleep when the job is done.' He grinned. 'If this plays out, you can start the crews working day after tomorrow.'

'I look forward to hearing good news,' Mack said.

Cobb left to get a short rest and Mack sent one of his security men to locate the foreman he wanted. He returned to his half-eaten meal, but had lost his interest in food.

'Two nights and a full day,' he mused to Mrs Peterson, unable to quell his worries. 'Then struggling to evade a pack of men from behind and another three or more in front of him. Look what I've done to the best employee I've ever had.'

'It was his choice to try this on his own,' she said mildly. 'He should have sent word back. He could have kept watch and waited until he had a small army of men.'

'At what risk to Miss Ekhard?' Mack queried. 'The kidnappers might have moved her. She might have been exposed to gunfire if it came to an all-out battle.' He heaved a weary sigh. 'No, the fault of this is on me. I should have allowed Brock to repay the money he lacked out of our future earnings. He would have gladly paid interest for the chance. But no, I allowed him to offer up his daughter as payment. I'm responsible for her life. Somehow, I have to make this right.'

Mrs Peterson stepped over and put a consoling hand on his shoulder. 'You're a good man, Mr Mackintosh. The wedding was no blackmail scheme, it was a business arrangement. Besides, you deserve a little happiness in your life.'

Mack looked at her and felt a measure of anxiety and fear dissipate. This lady was more than his housekeeper and cook, she was a friend, a confidant.

'You're a genteel and caring woman, Mrs Peterson. I wish there was something I could do for you.'

'You've given me a home, a job, and I feel more like a sister or aunt, rather than a servant. You've treated me better than anyone I've ever known before in my life. I am happy to be a part of your life's work.'

The foreman entered and the private moment between them was shattered. Mack began to instruct him in what was needed. He asked for volunteers, but offered to pay each of them a hundred-dollar bonus for their service. That pretty much insured that every man able to walk would volunteer. Cobb would be able to pick the best of the lot.

CHAPTER NINE

From an elevated vantage point, Bolt surveyed the trail he had taken. It was along a deer path. Rather than wander out in the open, deer would usually find a route that hid them from predators. This particular trail ran along the upper side of the canyon, near the wall, high on the hillside, but out of sight of anyone below. He wished there had been time to pack more food. The one can of beans they had shared that morning was not very filling. As each of their three-man party had packed for only a day or so, there had been very little stowed away to eat. He had to save the other tins of peaches and beans for the evening meal. That left only a handful of beef and venison jerky to get them through the day.

Rising up to his full height and easing a couple steps up the side of the hill, he was able to look down the expansive gorge and take inventory of the six riders. Only five were on horses now, with the sixth following their tracks on foot. Ariette was sitting on the ground, with her chin resting on her knees. She was working very hard to keep up, but her strength was beginning to wane.

Bolt dug out a strip of dried beef and handed it to her. 'Chew on this for a bit. It's kind of like food.'

The girl managed a jaded smile. 'Yes, I've had jerky many times before.'

'Well, there is store-bought jerky and home-made. This stuff could be used to patch a stone wall. I swear, Deek must have cut this from an old pair of boots.'

She managed a weary smile at his jest.

'You need to slip over to that next hollow and stay real low,' Bolt told her. 'I'm going to slow down our pursuit and things might become more lively.'

Ariette rose to her feet and took a step up the hill, far enough for her to be able to see the basin floor. She ducked back quickly and threw Bolt a terrified look.

'There are at least a half-dozen men down there! You can't expect to shoot them all before they get us?'

Bolt exhibited a false bravado for her sake. 'Just like laying track,' he told her calmly. 'Can't toss down a pair of rails and start the train rolling. Have to first level the ground and put down ties. Our main concern is to stay out of rifle range until we reach a point in this canyon that is closest to the direction we want to go. Until then, I intend to keep them fellers as far away as possible.'

'Couldn't we just hide?' she asked. 'They might go right past us.'

'They've got a man tracking us on foot. He would know if we tried something like that.' With a grim resolve he added, 'And he's almost to the deer trail we took. I don't want him where I can't see him.'

The girl did not hide her apprehension. 'Please be careful, Bolt,' she warned him. It was a nice gesture, but pointless under the circumstances. Then she began to edge her way down into the hollow he had indicated.

Bolt took up a set position behind a calf-sized boulder. He adjusted the distance on the open-sight and decided there was not enough breeze to worry about allowing for windage. With a round in the chamber, he placed the rifle against his shoulder, rested his elbow against the top of the boulder to steady his aim, then sighted down the barrel. He had been too young to fight in the war between the Union and the Confederacy, but he had done some Indian fighting and a great deal of hunting. His father had given him a gun when he was eight and expected him to provide rabbits, sage hens and other fowl. At twelve he had a pony and was able to hunt larger game. When he had bagged an antelope, deer or elk, he would drag it home behind his horse. By sixteen Bolt had earned a job with the railroad, supplying meat for the workers. One thing he had learned was how to hit what he was shooting at.

As for the men following, they had attacked a stage and killed an unarmed driver, along with Ariette's bodyguard. As for the kidnapping, that was a sin against all laws of decency. Any man who abducted a child or woman by force deserved to take a long step with a short rope securely about their neck. Bolt suppressed his usual compassion for mankind. This was not a time for humanity, it was a time for retribution and protection.

You'll never lay a hand on this young lady again, he vowed to himself, *not so long as I have a breath left in my body!*

Selecting the man doing the tracking, Bolt estimated the distance was about 1,000 yards. It was a difficult distance, as he was shooting slightly downhill. He lowered the sight range to about 800 yards to compensate, then took careful aim at the top of the man's head. He held his breath and lightly squeezed the trigger.

Mortimer stopped his horse, impatient with Handy's tracking skills. Yeah, the two fugitives were on foot, but they could only go one way. Once it was determined the pair were headed deeper into the canyon, they should have been able to run them down in a matter of minutes. There was no need to trace every single footprint.

Handy yelped like a stepped-on dog and spun completely around. His legs started pumping, as if he was going to make a dash back down the canyon. Instead, he pitched forward and plowed a furrow in the dirt with his chin and nose.

While Mortimer was trying to make sense of his bizarre reaction, a distant boom echoed off the walls.

'Duck!' Ethan cried, leaning low over the saddle and neck-reining his horse for cover. The other four started moving, but Clyde's horse buckled under him. As he and the animal both slammed into the earth, a second shot resounded across the basin.

'He's a long way up the canyon,' Wily shouted. 'I saw the smoke from his second shot.'

Mortimer jumped to the ground, holding the reins of his horse. He kept behind a cluster of rocks and checked to see that his sons and Ethan had all taken cover.

'You all right, son?' he called to Clyde.

'Killed my hoss, Pa,' came the reply. 'But he missed me.'

'Can you get a shot at him, Wily?' Mortimer called.

'Looks a half-mile away – uphill to boot,' Wily answered. 'Eagle-eye is the one with the buffalo gun. Ain't no way any of our rifles can reach that far.'

'We can work up that-away,' Ethan volunteered. 'Have to move from one bit of cover to the next. Don't give him time to aim. Run and drop, run and drop.'

Mortimer gnashed his teeth, seething with a helpless frustration. 'If'n we do that, he can keep moving ahead of us all morning. We won't get in range until we reach the end of the canyon.'

'Who's going to ride out in the open, big brother? The guy just proved he knows how to shoot.'

Mortimer still held the reins of his horse, so he

tied the straps to a nearby sagebrush and crawled over to Handy's body. He had been hit in the middle of the chest; the wound had been fatal. It was probable that Handy's physical reaction had been sheer instinct. He probably didn't even realize he'd been shot.

'We might be able to ride hard and fast,' Wily suggested. 'Zigzag and stay low on the saddle. From that distance he'd have a heck of a time hitting one of us.'

Mortimer looked at Ethan. 'What do you think?'

'Sounds like it might work. That fellow has to keep the gal safe, so he's likely going to keep inching along until he finds a place they can scale the cliff and get out of the canyon.'

'He's right, Pa,' Clyde put in. 'He gets over the top of the hill, we will have to ride all the way around to catch up. Take us half a day to find them again.'

'OK everyone, grab up the reins of your horses. Clyde, you catch up Handy's steed. When I give the word, we swing up and take off quick as fast as you can ride. Weave back and forth every few feet and we'll go as far as them two pinyon trees yonder. That's a hundred yards or so. When we get there, dismount and take cover. We'll spread out again and see if we can flush that coyote out into the open.'

Bolt watched the men, waiting for their next move. He observed them as they gathered up their horses. Once they took up the reins, he took aim. At such a distance, he couldn't make out any distinctive features. However, he knew he couldn't let them get too close. It would be impossible to climb the canyon wall if he and the girl had to dodge bullets every foot of the way.

Suddenly, all five riders rose up and swung up on the backs of their mounts. He saw their strategy at once. They dashed along the basin floor, then, after a short distance, each rider yanked his horse in a new direction. It was a trick that the Indians had used for years. He picked a target and waited for his next turn. He judged the next few feet the horse would cover and led both rider and horse. As the man jerked the reins to one side, he anticipated where he would end up and pulled the trigger.

The bullet arrived a split second before the man could change direction again. He jerked from being hit and, still holding the reins, yanked his horse's head around sharply. The result was both of them tumbled to the ground. The horse rolled on top of the rider, before regaining its feet. It then took several steps away from the immobile outlaw, shook its mane, and wandered over to nibble at a patch of buffalo grass.

The single shot shocked the other horsemen into action. They halted their animals and hit the ground, scrambling for cover. By the time Bolt had chambered a new round, there were no visible targets.

'Let's move,' he instructed Ariette. 'Keep to the deer trail and get going. I'll be right behind you.'

116

She threw him a fearful glance. 'Are they still coming?'

'I gave them two good reasons to rethink their situation. We should have a few minutes before we need to worry about them.'

Ariette was struggling with each step from the blisters on her feet. She actually groaned in an effort to get her tired, aching muscles to respond. Gritting her teeth, she began to move at a decent pace.

Bolt looked far ahead and espied a likely route up the mountain. It appeared steep and treacherous in places, but it appeared accessible all the way to the top of the ridge. As the possible escape was a long way off, he would have time to set up a second ambush to hold the Voight bunch at bay. With a little luck and proper planning, the girl could start the climb on her own and he would cover her until the going got tough. Then he could join her and help get her the rest of the way . . . hopefully before the outlaw gang caught up to them.

There were several hours of daylight left. They needed to manage as much separation as possible. If the outlaws were within rifle range, they would be forced to wait for the cover of darkness. That idea was not good, because the killers would be able to close in while he was climbing and vulnerable to attack.

CHAPTER TEN

Mortimer crawled to the fallen man. After a few moments, he swore vehemently.

'Kilt Handy! Now my brother is dead!'

'That's it for me,' Wily spoke up. 'I ain't gonna ride after a man who can shoot like him. I didn't kill or kidnap nobody. I just come along for the money.' He snorted his contempt. 'Ain't no one getting paid around here except in lead!'

'You yella snake!' Mortimer shouted. 'What about Handy and your other pal?'

'Never liked neither one enough to get myself shot over. I'll be seeing you.'

Even as Mortimer swore at him, Wily swung up onto the back of his horse. Without looking back, he took off at a hard run, headed for the mouth of the canyon.

Clyde and Rich made their way over to their father. He was sitting on his heels and staring up the canyon, his teeth on a bind, jaw clenched in hate.

'What now, Pa?' Rich asked.

'We leave the blasted horses and go after that mangy mutt on foot. We hug the side of the hill, stick right on his tracks, and use every bit of cover along the way. Time is on our side.'

'Corner him and he'll fight,' Clyde said. 'Might get another of us killed.'

Mortimer shook his head. 'We don't offer him a shot. One of us will be as high up the side of the hill as possible, another down low, and one on his tracks. If he tries to get a shot off, one of us will be in a position to shoot first.'

'I get your plan,' Clyde joined in. 'We move in from three levels at the same time. Ain't no way he can set himself for a shot without being seen.'

Mortimer patted the shoulder of Ethan's body in farewell, then put a resolute stare on his sons.

'Picket your mounts. Grab your canteens and something to eat. This might take the rest of the day, but we'll get him.' With a controlled rage: 'We'll get them both!'

After a time along their path, Ariette discovered a puddle of water, trapped in the hollow of a rock. It wasn't something they could drink, but it was useful. They took a short break and Ariette removed her shoes and socks. She quickly washed and soaked her sore feet for a few minutes.

While the girl was treating her blisters, Bolt moved to a higher position and checked on the pursuit. One man was obviously directing the movement of the three. He had seen the one rider leave,

119

but from the hollering and harsh tone of voice that followed after him, it was evident the man was not going for help. No, he was running for his life. The number to their rear was now half of what had started.

'Can you see them?' Ariette asked.

'Yes. They are moving like Indians now. On foot, first one, then another – short distances, from cover to cover. No chance for a clear shot.'

'Then they are gaining on us?'

Bolt grunted. He leaned the heavy Sharps gun against a rock and turned to face the girl.

'No. Being so careful takes a lot of effort and time. We're still a long way in front of them.'

'It looks like we're getting near the end of the canyon.'

'There's a good-looking route for climbing not too far ahead. We'll get high up as quickly as we can. There is an easier-looking route at the head of the canyon, but the men following might know about it. If so, they'll expect us to try and climb out there. With luck we might get up this rocky fissure and reach the top before they can get within range to shoot.'

Ariette patted her feet dry with the hem of her riding skirt and began to put on her socks. Bolt noticed the rusty-colored bloodstains and could not help but admire her grit.

'You might be a lady, but you've got the heart of a pioneer woman,' he praised. 'Nary a complaint, with little water or food, and your feet have to be killing you.'

'The difficulty I'm in at the moment is a product of my own doing. If I was to curse anyone for my situation, it would be myself.'

'You didn't ask to marry Big Mack.'

'No, but I did accept it as my duty.' She made a face. 'That is, until I was faced with the reality of my situation. I tried to think of my family first, I really did.' She sighed. 'The thing is, a person only gets one life. It's terribly selfish of me, but I don't want to forfeit my one and only chance at happiness in a marriage contract I had no say about.'

'I understand completely, Miss Ekhard.'

She gave him an odd look. 'I believe you do.'

Bolt lifted one shoulder in a shrug. 'If I was your father, I could never have agreed to such a thing. After all, it isn't as if he's going to lose his interest in the railroad. It was only that he would no longer be an equal partner. When you look at the past couple years, while I've been working with Big Mack, I've never even met your father. Seems to me, Mack is the senior partner with or without the percentage being equal. He's the one on the job, the man making the decisions, the one seeing the work gets done.'

'That's true,' Ariette agreed. 'Father once mentioned that Mack earned ten percent of his investment by managing the railroad. Perhaps that is the reason my father wanted to have this wedding; he might have felt guilty about not doing his share of the actual work.'

As Bolt watched the girl gingerly put on her shoes, he made a decision. 'I'll make a promise to you, Miss Ekhard. If we get though this in one piece, I will stand up for you. I'll tell Mack you would be proud to work for him, do whatever you can to pay your father's debt, but you don't wish to marry him.'

Ariette's eyes broadened in surprise. Her lips parted, but no words were formed.

'The thing is, I know Mack as well as if he was my own father. Once I talk to him he isn't going to demand you marry him. I know he'll let you out of the promise.'

Ariette came to her feet – wincing from the pain, but standing within arm's length of Bolt.

'You would do that?' she asked, breathlessly, as if she didn't believe such an approach was possible.

'Like I said, I've spent a lot of time with Mack. I know the man's character. He would never force you to marry him. I wager, he'll release you without saying a bad word about you or your father.'

Ariette abruptly came forward, threw her arms around Bolt's neck and hugged him tightly. Before he had a chance to enjoy the embrace, she began to sob against his chest.

What the hey? he wondered. *I thought this was what she wanted. Why the tears?*

Feeling awkward and uncomfortable, he stood feebly with his hands at his sides. A lame response to her reaction, but he had no idea how to deal with a weeping woman. Especially one he had just offered to help.

'I'm sorry,' Ariette murmured, pulling back from the impulsive embrace. 'It's just that . . . well, no one has ever done the things for me that you have. You saved my life, you rescued me from kidnappers, and now you are willing to stand up to your boss and my father on my behalf. You've shown me more consideration in the short while I've known you than anyone has for me in my entire life.'

'Every person ought to have a chance to make their own fate,' he replied. 'I mean, without love and happiness, what's the use of living?'

She smiled, her eyes still glistening from her tears. 'I agree wholeheartedly.'

'You ready to go?'

Remarkably, the girl laughed, practically giddy. 'Now that I have a reason to climb, you just try and keep up.'

Bolt smiled at her renewed enthusiasm. 'Let's get moving.'

Eagle-eye studied the ground and walked in a short circle. Abe and Butcher Voight remained aboard their horses, clueless as to what he was doing.

'Can't be any doubt,' he told the brothers. 'The horse with the wounded rider made a false trail and then headed for town.'

'Them folks in Lost Bend know not to hide anyone from our kin,' Abe jeered.

'Be a waste of time for us to run them down,' Eagle-eye said, mounting up on his horse. 'We don't care about those two jokers. It's the girl we want. We get her back, we find a new place to hole up and still get our money.'

'But they will know who we are,' Butcher cried.

'Makes no never-mind, boys. We keep moving until we arrange a ransom exchange, then split up the money and leave this part of the territory. With that much cash, we can go wherever we want.'

'Man's right,' Abe said. 'We can head for Colorado or Utah ... even Montana. We ain't leaving nothing behind here in Wyoming.'

'So what do we do now?' Butcher wanted to know. 'The third man and the girl must have gone up the canyon. That means Uncle Mortimer will catch them. Shucks! They might have them already.'

'Can't be sure of that,' Eagle-eye warned. 'Remember, we heard a single shot a few minutes back; it came from a big gun and the sound carried for miles. I'm the only one of our group with a buffalo gun, so that means the man with the girl has the same type weapon. He can keep Mortimer and the others a long way off if he's any good.'

'Keep talking,' Abe encouraged.

'So, with the wounded man being taken to Lost Bend, they can't possibly get any help for a day or two. Figure one man is out of the fight. The second has to ride all the way to Mackintosh's end of the railroad. That's going a long way in the wrong direction. By the time he can round up help and get back, it will be sometime tomorrow.'

'I agree with your figuring,' Abe concurred.

'So we know our pair of runners is the girl and

one man. That fellow sure ain't gonna risk getting the girl killed by a stray bullet. He must figure on climbing out of the canyon, once they reach the end.'

'There is a trail out at the box end of the canyon. It's too rugged for a horse, but a man on foot could climb out.' Abe guessed the plan: 'We can be waiting for them on this side.'

'You got it,' Eagle-eye agreed. 'While the guy and the girl are looking over their shoulders for the pursuit from the canyon, we'll be sitting there atop the hill waiting for them.'

'Providing they come over the top where you expect,' Butcher tossed out a negative thought. 'They might try and escape before they get trapped. What then?'

Eagle-eye did some thinking. 'That's a good point. We'll have to stay far enough down below the mountain crest to move one way or the other. We can split up and cover three points, say . . . a hundred yards or so apart, but where each of us can see one of the others. Soon as one of us spots them, or we hear where he is shooting, we converge together and take out the man with the gun. The girl won't put up any fight. I seriously doubt she's ever shot a gun in her life.'

'It's a good plan,' Abe said. 'Let's get going. With the rough country betwixt here and there, it'll be close to dark before we reach the range of hills beyond the canyon.'

*

Mack shook hands with Cobb and wished him luck.
Then he stood at the back door of his luxury rail car
and watched the man lead a dozen riders away at a
lope. Cobb had always been brash and a braggart,
but it was innocuous and usually meant to entertain.
This time his prowess would be tested. Bolt and
Ariette's lives depended on his ability to find them.

'I prepared some cold sandwiches,' Mrs Peterson
spoke up from behind him. 'That way, we can eat
whenever you feel up to it.'

Mack rotated about to look at her. Never had he
known such an attentive, thoughtful woman. She
never ceased worrying about him, even to the point
that he had given up his cigars and seldom drank
more than a glass of wine at nights. She was more
than his servant, she was his nursemaid, his conscience and, not infrequently, his counsel.

'You deserve so much more than I've given you,
Regina,' he said quietly, solemnly. Her brows arched
and her oddly inviting lips parted in surprise. He
had never before addressed her by her first name.

'I've been blinded by ambition and the desire to
regain my youth and possibly have a child of my
own. My self-absorption has caused me to endanger
an innocent young lady and a man I would gladly
call my son. Bolt is out there fighting for his life,
trying to save a girl who is less than half my age. And
what brought this about? My intending to make
Ariette a child bride and mother to a son or daughter of my own!'

'It's something you've wanted for a long time,

something most everyone wants . . . a real family.'

Mack shook his head. 'Yes, and look at the cost! Bolt might die defending the girl I'm forcing into wedlock.' He snorted his contempt. 'To tell the truth, I don't blame her for running away.'

'But you're a good man,' Mrs Peterson argued. 'You would make her a fine husband, and you would be a good father to a child.'

He waved a dismissive hand. 'The selfish, silly notions of a middle-aged man.'

'Then you've changed your mind? You don't want Miss Ekhard for your wife?'

'I already feel like a married man,' he said, staring at her with a meaningful look. 'You've been like a wife to me these past two years, Regina. I think I would like to make our arrangement permanent.' He smiled. 'Maybe with a few added benefits . . . if you're agreeable to my proposal.'

He saw a mixture of joy and surprise in her face, yet she remained steadfast. 'This could be a weak moment on your part. You've yet to meet Miss Ekhard. You might have a change of heart.'

Mack reached out and placed his hands gently on Regina's shoulders. 'I would very much like to kiss you. But I need to know this is something you want, too.'

Instead of replying in words, Regina moved into his arms and placed her lips to his. It was delightful to hold her close and Mack knew it could have never felt so right with the youthful Ariette.

*

127

Bolt kept watch until the girl had reached a steep-walled section and needed his help to climb higher. A few clouds were overhead and a cool breeze had begun to blow. He held the rifle up, searching for a final shot, but the three remaining hunters were taking no chances. They kept low to the ground and he only occasionally spotted a man's head. Even then, it popped up for but a second and was gone. They were moving on their hands and knees, with one following their tracks and the other two hugging the lower side of the hill.

Judging the rock-jutted stairway they had to climb, he worried about being exposed to the guns below. Once he was involved in scaling the sheer cliff face, return fire would be difficult or impossible. The positive side was the hunters would have to shoot with care. They would need the girl alive for any ransom exchange. On the opposite side, he didn't want to endanger the girl any more than necessary. If the Voight bunch got within shooting distance, he would have to try and get her to safety, then do what he could to stop them from following.

'I'm as far as I can go,' Ariette called down, her voice as hushed as possible, yet loud enough so he could hear. 'You'll have to lift me high enough so I can get over this next ledge.'

He stuck his head through the buckskin rifle-strap and slipped it over one shoulder. Then he hurried to the crevice and began to climb. It took only a couple minutes to reach Ariette's position.

'I think, with your help, I can get up on this

protruding shelf,' she said. 'But you'll have to climb ahead of me on that next one.' She pointed at a large projecting ridge, another twenty or so feet up the rocky face. It offered only a handhold or two and Bolt would have to scale it like a monkey. She added: 'I'm pretty sure I won't be able to manage that one.'

As their route had been chosen, there was no alternative but to continue the ascent. Bolt took up a position where he could lift the girl high enough for her to put her foot into a crack in the stone face. From there, she was able to grab hold of the ledge and pull herself up. Bolt helped to push her up, then followed quickly, being more agile and with a longer reach. He grunted from the effort, but got onto the stone shelf with Ariette.

'They've seen us,' she cried. 'Look!'

Bolt barely had room to turn, but he saw the three men were on their feet, dashing to get their horses. They would be in a position to shoot at them in no time.

'Quick!' he said. 'We need to reach that next ledge. It extends out quite a ways and should give us some cover.'

Ariette was not conditioned for this hard physical labor, but she responded with what strength she had left. She climbed the short way to the overhang and waited for Bolt to go past her. He shrugged the rifle-strap over his head and handed the weapon to her. Next, he jumped up high enough to grab hold of the rock. It was a chore that caused his muscles to cry out from the strain, but Bolt pulled himself up until he could see over the jagged outcrop. With a lunge, he stretched out and wrapped his fingers around a notch in the stone. Grunting from the difficulty, he pulled his body up and onto the ledge.

There was no time to catch his breath. He found the perch was several feet deep and twice as long. Being part of the jagged wall, it was plenty strong enough to support the weight of both of them. He leaned over and looked down at the waiting girl.

'Pass the barrel of the rifle to me and get a firm grip on the stock. It's not loaded, so use the trigger guard if you have to. I'll pull you up until I can reach your wrists. Try to use your feet to help climb the wall.'

She didn't hesitate, firmly grasping the stock of the rifle and lifting it up until he could get both hands on it. Bolt jammed his heel against a knobby protrusion and, using it for leverage, heaved and tugged until Ariette's arms appeared. Then he kept her steady and grabbed hold of her wrist. She let go of the rifle, which he set aside, then he dragged her up next to him.

Sitting back, his lungs were on fire and his arms and shoulders burned from the strenuous exertion. Ariette simply lay on her back and sucked in great gulps of air. They had little time to rest, as hoofbeats reached Bolt's ears. He grabbed the Spencer, loaded it at once, and took up a shooter's position. Sitting with his knees up, he braced his elbows against the inside of his legs and took aim.

One of the men yelled a warning and they all darted behind the lower foothill, out of sight. Bolt cursed his not being ready. If he could have gotten one more of them, they might have decided catching him and Ariette wasn't worth the price.

Casting a glance at the rocky staircase they had yet to climb, he saw it was much easier going for the next little way. Leaning back, he tried to spot a good hiding-place. He needed to locate a hollow or overhang that would protect them from gunfire from below.

'Can you make it a little further?' he queried.

Jaded until the effort to speak was difficult, Ariette gave a slight nod. He helped her to her feet and she began to climb once more. Bolt remained where he was, ready to shoot if one of the trackers got careless. It didn't take long before he realized what the Voights were up to. They had split up and were moving to either side of his position. By flanking him, they could take turns shooting at him and keep him pinned down. Even if he had a good place to shoot from, the three men could maneuver around until one of them got a clear shot.

Rather than wait for the trap to be readied, Bolt strapped on the rifle and began to climb. He would keep close to Ariette and hope to find a decent bit of cover. If they managed to get high enough up the mountain and found a defensible position, they could wait for nightfall to finish the climb.

CHAPTER ELEVEN

Cobb reached the fork where he intended to turn toward the mountain range. He called one of the men over and sent him to inform Proctor of what was going on. It was still ten miles to the leeward side of the box canyon and there were many washes and gullies that made for slow going.

'You sure you know where that canyon ends?' asked the Dutchman, who moved up to ride alongside of him. 'Even the surveyors never went this far south.'

'Hell, son,' Cobb replied, 'a few years back, my horse was shot out from under me by a Cheyenne war party. They come after my hair and I was forced into that very canyon.'

'How'd you get away?'

'As it happened, a herd of buffalo was wintering there. I swung up on the back of the biggest bull in the herd and led a stampede right thought the middle of them red devils. Scared them so bad they gave me the name *Big Buffalo Rider*, and never bothered me again.'

'Sounds like quite a tale,' the man replied drily. Then, with a skyward glance, 'Looks like some clouds moving in; likely make it dark earlier than usual.'

'Be better for Bolterfeld,' Cobb said. 'If there's no moon, it'll be harder for the gang of cutthroats to see him and the girl.'

'Harder for us too.'

Cobb laughed. 'I'll lead you right to them, no matter how dark it gets.'

'Yeah? And how's that?'

'Purr'fume,' he answered, intentionally dragging out the epithet. 'That there gal wears the sweetest purr'fume I ever smelt.'

'You got that close to her, did you?'

'Had her riding back of me during our getaway, sonny boy,' Cobb bragged. 'Tell you what, she feels real fine when hugging you tight.'

'Better not be saying something like that in front of Big Mack,' the Dutchman warned. 'He might get jealous.'

'You keep it to yourself,' Cobb threatened. 'That was one of them there private moments betwixt a man and a woman. It ain't meant to be shared.' With a grin, 'It's to be savored by a man like me, and it's something the woman can only dream about on a cold and lonely night.'

The man grunted his incredulity and asked: 'How much further?'

'We'll keep a good pace till dusk. After that, we need to keep an eye out for the three jackals that tried to cut me and Deek off from town. We had to sit quiet and let them ride past.' He shook his head. 'I'd have emptied their saddles there and then, but Deek was bleeding and I couldn't risk him dying on me.'

'Three men won't be a problem, not for a dozen of us.'

'Yeah, well, I don't want any of you getting shot up. We'll do this careful and get the job done without losing anyone.'

'Providing Bolterfeld can keep the girl until we get to him.'

'Next to me, he's the most capable man on Big Mack's payroll. He'll keep the girl safe . . . even if it costs him his life.'

The darkness of the sky erupted in a violent thunder, and hail slapped and screamed off the nearby rocks. This storm wasn't Nature's doing, but the result of blasting rifles and flying lead. The three men below had worked to optimum positions: two high up the hillside – one on either flank, and one below. The shooters must have expected that Bolt would put the girl in a secure place, as dozens of bullets ricocheted and caromed off the stone walls and the rocks protecting his location.

Fragments struck Bolt from the extended volley, nicking his neck, left shoulder and back. He had no chance to return fire during the assault and decided the chance of a rebound bullet was the only plan from the three shooters. Then it suddenly went quiet, other than for the ringing in Bolt's ears.

'Whoever you are up there, mister,' a man called from below, 'We're giving you one chance to send the girl down. We don't want to kill her, but we will if we have to.'

Bolt automatically glanced at Ariette, but he knew her answer. She was wedged down in a concave opening, a nook where he had piled rocks and dirt to provide her with a safe place to remain during any shooting. The sun was down and it would be dark soon. The heavy fire from below told him the three kidnappers knew their time was running out.

'What say you?' the same man bellowed again. 'You lookin' to watch that girl get hit by a ricochet and maybe die?'

'Help is on its way,' Bolt called back. 'You better run while you can.'

His words caused another storm, equal in intensity to the first round. Bolt kept his face down and winced from chips of rock pelting his back and legs. This time, he was ready when the shooting stopped. He rose up with the Sharps and quickly scanned the place where he figured the one on his left would be hiding. A head bobbed and he squeezed off a round.

There was an immediate yelp and the attacker on that side scrambled to better cover. Bolt didn't think he'd done much damage to the man, but it was a reminder that they would be fools to try and rush his position.

'Sing out, Clyde,' the man from below shouted.

135

'It ain't bad, Pa. Just a crease below my hip. I can tend to it myself.'

Bolt knew *Pa* was Mortimer Voight. He decided to talk directly to him.

'Word is out on your family,' he directed his voice to the man below. 'If you harm this young lady there won't be a place in the world for you to hide. Your kidnapping involves the railroad. That means your names will be turned over to the Pinkerton detectives. You know their motto – *the eye that never sleeps.* They will hunt down each and every one of you.'

'We'll have enough money to leave the country,' the man shouted back. 'Ain't no one gonna ever find us.'

'Lie to yourself, Voight, but don't bother lying to me. You are signing your own death warrants by sticking around. You run now, maybe the Pinkertons don't get involved. You've paid a price in lives for kidnapping the girl. Mackintosh might figure that's enough.'

'Is he telling it straight, Pa?' A new voice came from the opposite side of Bolt's position. 'Are we going up against the Pinkertons?'

'Hush up, boy,' the old man wailed. 'You want that sharp-eyed polecat shooting your way?'

'Think about it, Voight,' Bolt repeated the warning. 'Anything happens to this girl and you'll never be able to run far enough.'

'Once you're dead, won't be no one to point a finger at us. The girl has never seen our faces.'

'It's your choice,' Bolt threatened him. 'Run or die.'

'Enough stalling, mister. We give you a chance to protect the girl from harm. If you don't take it, you'll be the one responsible for her getting hurt or kilt.'

Bolt again gave Ariette a look.

'I'm staying with you, Bolt,' she declared. 'No matter what!'

He couldn't help but grin. 'Look at the city gal! You've become a true frontier woman these last couple of days.'

'I only wish we would have had time for you to teach me to shoot.'

'Not room on this ledge for more than one,' he replied to that. 'You stay hunkered down so I don't have to worry about you. That's the best thing you can do to help at the moment.'

'Whatever you say, Bolt,' she acquiesced. 'Just don't get hit by one of their bullets.'

He gave a confident tip of his head and said: 'There's very little overhang to bounce their bullets off, and only a few rocks they can hit from below or either side. They will have to get above me to get a shot, and I can watch out and prevent that.'

A single pebble rolling down the hill was his only warning. Bolt jerked his head around and stared up at the top of the mountain crest. Three figures were silhouetted against the sky.

He rolled backwards as a new barrage of bullets rained down from above. His only escape from the deadly hail was to put his back against Ariette's improvised bunker.

Setting aside the Sharps rifle, Bolt grabbed his Colt and pressed back against the acclivity, standing ready to fire.

'They're above us too?' Dread and fear laced Ariette's question.

Bolt responded softly, hiding his own anxiety. 'Three of them, but they can't get to us, not without showing themselves.'

'Above us, below us, and to either side,' she summed up. 'Bolt! Maybe I should surrender to them. They might let you live.'

'No matter what that old man promises, they can't afford to leave either of us alive. Fighting back is the only chance we have.'

He knelt down and took hold of the girl's hand. 'It will be completely dark in a few minutes,' he said, squeezing the diminutive fist in a show of faith. 'It'll make it difficult for them to move about, and I've got exceptionally keen hearing. If they try and get to us, I'll cut their number down in one big hurry.'

Bolt hated to exaggerate, facing such odds, but he wanted to reassure the girl. If she panicked and lost control, it could mean the end of them both. She had to believe he was up to the task of defending her . . . even if it was a near impossibility.

Eagle-eye kept the Voight brothers ready to either side, squatted low behind cover. He had hoped to get a clear shot at the man below, but the guy had spooked. Now they had to dig him out, like a badger in a hole – a chore that was equally dangerous.

Down below, Mortimer moved out far enough for him to be seen, but still remaining safe from the gunman up on the rock shelf. The old man pointed to the positions of his other two shooters. Eagle-eye lifted his arms, palms out and facing up, a silent question as to where the rest of the men were at. The old man shook his head.

Hot-dang!

Eagle-eye was stunned. The man in the rocks had either killed, wounded or driven off three of Voight's bunch. He moved a little to one side and then the other, able to see that the two remaining shooters were Mortimer's sons. That meant Handy and Wily were either dead or gone, along with Ethan Voight.

'How we going to flush him out?' Abe wanted to know. 'Ain't no good boulders up this way for starting a rock slide.'

'Yeah,' Butcher joined in. 'And I don't see Pa down there. Where's he at?'

Eagle-eye took a quick survey of the landscape, looking for safe routes that would put him or one of the boys in position to kill the rescuer. But both sides were openly exposed – consisting of dirt and shale rock, with only an occasional bush or small pinyon for cover. The rocky ravine between him and the girl narrowed to only a couple feet deep as it reached the summit of the mountain, so it didn't offer good cover for a direct approach.

'Looks as if Clyde and Rich are about as far up the hillside as they can get,' he said to the two boys. 'And it would be suicide to try and get down the hill far enough to get a shot at that fellow.'

'You think he's that good with a gun?'

'Can't you count, Abe?' he growled. 'Half of the men who started out chasing him are missing.'

'Uncle Mortimer!' Abe shouted loud enough for his voice to carry down to the canyon floor. 'Where's our pa?'

The man didn't have to answer. He lowered his head and avoided looking up at him.

'Ah, no!' Butcher whined. 'That dirty, no-good, railroader killed our pa.'

'This kidnapping has gone to hell in a bucket,' Abe lamented. 'None of us were supposed to get dead over this.'

'Act like a man,' Eagle-eye snarled at the two brothers. 'First, we deal with the joker who killed your pa. After that, you can cry in your beer until the snow flies.'

'How we gonna get at him?' Abe said, sniffing to prevent tears. 'There's no place to move along the top of this mountain where we can get a clean shot.'

Eagle-eye surveyed the area below and saw where the wind had blown a good many tumbleweeds. The grass was also dry and there were some sagebrush and a thicket or two of oak brush. He took a moment to test the slight breeze, then waved to Mortimer. Once the man was looking at him, he pointed to the nearby pile of brush. He made a few

140

gestures and Mortimer realized what he had in mind.

'All right,' he said, once Mortimer was on the move. 'Gather all of the sticks, brush and kindling you can round up. We're going to head down the draw, get as close as we can, then strike a match. We'll push everything that will burn down the hill ahead of us. We'll either smoke those two out of hiding or we'll roast them alive.'

The sun had set and Bolt and Ariette shared what might be their last meal. By the time they finished, it was nearly dark. Bolt moved carefully and risked quick peeks around the rocks, trying to assess the strategy of the attackers. He spotted piles of bush being placed at the top of the ravine. Checking down below, he saw that Mortimer had begun to make a second mound of tumbleweeds and brushwood. Bolt saw the plan and it was a good one.

He might have attempted to get off a shot with the Sharps, but the two boys were watching from either side. Even a second glance at Mortimer earned him a bullet a few inches from his head. *Pin him down, start fires above and below, then feed that fire and keep moving closer.* The stuff below would never reach Bolt and Ariette, but the smoke would make it difficult to see. As for the fire above, if they found enough tinder, they could push the fire ahead of them and eventually shove it right down on top of his position.

'What is it?' Ariette asked. 'What are they doing?'

141

'They intend to smoke us out.'

She flicked her eyes about, searching for anything that would burn. 'We're safe, aren't we? I mean, it's all rock here.'

'Yes, but they can come at us straight down from above and I won't be able to see them for the smoke and fire. If they shove a pile of burning brush down on top of us, we are going to get singed.'

In spite of his warning Ariette crawled out of her hole. Before he knew her design, she came into his arms. She clung tightly to him, as if trying to draw strength from his courage. This was a nightmare, worse than anything she had ever imagined.

'I'm sorry,' Bolt whispered softly in her ear. 'I've led you to a terrible fate.'

Ariette leaned back and looked up at him. 'None of this is your fault.' Her voice was firm and resolute. 'You've done everything humanly possible to save me. I am forever in your debt.'

'*Forever* might not be much longer,' he said. 'I can't shoot what I can't see. With six men surrounding us, we haven't much of a chance.'

'If we must die I'm thankful to be with you, Bolt,' she avowed, staring into his eyes. 'You're the kind of man I would have loved to spend my life with. You have honor, you're caring, you're a gentleman, you're. . . .'

Bolt leaned down and kissed her. It was a short contact, then he pulled back and grinned. 'See? I'm not such a gentleman after all.'

But she reciprocated by kissing him back. After a

few wondrous seconds, she leaned away and smiled up at him.

'To the contrary, it was very gentlemanly. You didn't force me to kiss you first.'

'Looks like I might live up to my name – Romeo and Juliet both died at the end of their story.'

'It was quite romantic – a romantic tragedy.'

'Well, Romeo and Ariette aren't going to take poison and go quietly. If I can hit another couple of them, they might decide our hides are too expensive.'

'Bolt,' she murmured, kissing him tenderly a second time. 'I would rather share these last minutes with you than have a full life married to a man I didn't love.'

'If we get out of this, I'll make sure I'm the only man you'll ever marry.'

'I like the sound of that, Bolt,' she said. 'If we survive this, we can be together for the rest of our lives.'

Bolt might have said something about them being in that very predicament. The *rest of their lives* might only be a few minutes. Instead, he stepped away from her and took a careful look at their position.

'The safest place for you is in your cubbyhole. When the fire gets close, I'll have to make my move. I don't want to worry about you getting hit by any stray bullets.'

'I'll do whatever you say,' she vowed. Then she placed a tender hand against his beard-stubbled

143

cheek. 'Just promise me you won't get killed.'

He managed a confident smile for her sake. 'No chance of that, Ariette. This will be a thrilling story to tell our grandkids. I don't intend to miss out on that.'

Ariette crawled into her pigeonhole and scooted down until there was hardly any of her showing. Bolt checked the loads in his pistol and picked up the Sharps. With the men above him working to build up their wall of fire, he slipped carefully over to where he had waited out the barrage from Mortimer and his two sons. Easing forward, he kept watch. He would use his ears to listen for the men coming down from above. As for the Voight boys on either side, they could no longer see him clearly in the dusk. Readying the rifle for use, he watched for the right moment to fire. If Mortimer had a match, he would be lit up the instant he brought the fire to life. An accurate shot just might cut the odds by one more.

Only six men between me and a wonderful life, he mused. 'Come on, boys,' he muttered under his breath, 'I've got a parting gift of lead for each of you!'

CHAPTER TWELVE

Cobb led the way, dodging brush, avoiding deep gullies and climbing ever upward to reach the far side of the canyon. They were getting close, but he had to move carefully, in case they ran into some of Voight's gang. He didn't want any of the men with him to get hurt, but there was little time for caution. Bolterfeld and the girl had been on foot and running for their lives for almost twenty-four hours. Even a capable man would only be able to outsmart an entire gang of cutthroats for so long. What good the rescue if they arrived to late?

'Say, Cobb,' a man he knew only as Winters spoke up. 'I smell smoke.'

'Me too!' Dutch whispered. 'Bolt wouldn't have lit a signal fire for us, do you think?'

Before Cobb could answer, the boom of a big gun split the night calm. It seemed to come from almost directly over the hill in front of them. He recognized it as his Sharps rifle. There was a few seconds' delay and then a host of guns opened up, cracking the serenity with a tidal wave of explosive gunfire.

'Let's go, men!' Cobb shouted. 'Ride as hard as you can and watch for anything that moves. I reckon Bolterfeld is hip-deep in flying bullets.'

The horses lunged and climbed for all they were worth. When they were played out, the men dismounted. Two stayed behind with the animals, while the rest of them grabbed their rifles and rushed up the hill on foot. The shooting continued, which was a good sign; it meant Bolt was still in the fight, but his time could be running out.

Cobb was suffering like a wind-broke horse as he topped the peak. It took only a moment to see the three men who were shooting just below.

'Nice of them to light a fire so we can see them,' Dutch panted at his side.

'Throw up your hands,' Cobb hollered a warning. 'You're surrounded!'

But all three turned to shoot at the new arrivals. As they swung about, Cobb commanded: 'Get 'em, men!'

Five or six of his men opened up on the trio, cutting them down like a row of targets.

No longer concerned with those three, Cobb moved to a higher spot. From there, he could see the canyon floor. Two blurry figures were near a second fire. It looked like there was a body lying on the ground too. The pair were obviously confused by the amount of shooting from up above.

'Winters,' he called the man over to him. 'Can you see to hit them two men down below?'

'Like pickin' cherries, Cobb,' came the reply. Then he took aim. Before he could fire his first round, two more men joined the pair, with their rifles raised.

The shooting was fast and deadly. In less than a minute, every visible man was down. Most had been hit more than once and not one was able to return fire. Cobb told Winters to help bring up the horses, while he and several others began the climb down the hillside.

When he reached the bodies of the three downed gang members, Cobb yelled: 'Shout out, missy! . . . Bolterfeld! Can you hear me?'

'Here,' came the high-pitched cry of a woman. 'Hurry!'

'A couple of you men, head on down to the basin floor and check on those *hombres*,' Cobb commanded, pointing out men for the chore. 'Dutch, you have a look-see at the three lying above us. Careful you don't approach anyone till you made certain they aren't holding a hideaway gun. Don't want none of us getting shot.'

Dutch left to do Cobb's bidding while the old scout and two remaining men continued to climb down to Bolt's position. The fires had died down, no longer being fed new brush or wood. It took a few minutes before Cobb circumnavigated the smoldering pockets of fire and reached the rocky shelf supporting Bolt and the girl.

'How is he, missy?' he asked, climbing onto the ledge and kicking a last smoking bush over the rocky lip. He moved to where the girl was sitting down. She had Bolt's head in her lap and had a folded piece of cloth pressed to his inner shoulder.

'He's been shot to pieces.' She sobbed the words. 'He said he got the one called Mortimer down on the canyon floor, and then there came a barrage of shooting. The men above were pushing down piles of burning rubbish, while the men to either side kept firing too. Bolt kept shooting back and kept the fire away until he heard you shout out for the attackers to surrender from atop the ridge. Then he collapsed.'

Cobb and the other two men were quick to assess Bolt's injuries. They dressed a wound near his hip, another on his forearm, and then worked on the shoulder. He bled freely from each puncture, but the bullets had missed the major arteries.

'We've done all we can,' Cobb told the men with him. 'One of you get a couple more men to help carry Bolterfeld, and the other tell Winters to prepare a travois. We stopped most of the bleeding, but he needs more care than we can give him here. Proctor has a surgeon working for him. Got kicked out of army for drinking, but can't blame him for that.' He gave a helpless shrug. 'I'm the one he was trying to drink under the table at the time.'

'What about the kidnappers?'

'Tell Dutch to take charge. Half of the men can stay here and gather them up – dead or alive. Round up their horses and take them all to Lost Bend. Tell Dutch I'll meet you and the boys there tomorrow so we can deal with the bodies and any of the varmints who pull through.'

Cobb recovered his Sharps, then waited until two men arrived to carry Bolt. It was slow going until they got out of the gorge. Once on the side of the hill, two more men came to help and the four of them worked quickly up the incline.

'How about you, missy?' Cobb asked her, once they were making the climb behind Bolt. 'How did you manage to not get hit?'

'I stayed put where Bolt told me. He had me buried in a hole where no bullets could touch me.' She gave a worried shake of her head. 'My fear was being roasted alive, when the men above us started to push the burning brush down on us. Bolt used the rifle and knocked most of it over the edge. Even after he was shot, he kept knocking the fire away.'

'Bolterfeld is rawhide tough,' Cobb told her. 'He'll shake off those little nicks in a coupla days.'

'Did you get all of the gang?'

'They were trapped in the light of their own fires. I doubt any of them survived.'

'Good thing you arrived when you did,' she said. 'Bolt's handgun was empty and he could barely stand up. We were seconds away from being killed.'

'*Just-in-time Cobb's* the name,' he joked. 'Had everything figured so that me and boys would arrive just in time.'

'Can you find the Proctor railroad line in the dark?'

'I can't see long distances for shucks, but I do see

149

nearly as well at night as during the day. I calculate it's no more'n twelve to fifteen mile to the end-of-tracks. We should be there in four or five hours.'

'But Bolt is bleeding!'

'We put stoppers in them there holes, missy. We'll shove a little red-eye and plenty of water down him – he'll make it.'

'How can you be sure?'

' 'Cause, little lady, I think you sure 'nuff stole his heart. For a prize like you, he won't give up the ghost. No siree!'

Bolt's world was one of jarring pain and a bumpy ride in the black of night. He relished the memory of the few rest stops, when Ariette's face would appear, staring down at him, speaking soft words like those of an angel. She had held his hand and caressed his face, wiping his brow with a damp cloth and putting a canteen to his lips.

One time he recalled the face had changed into Cobb's grizzled features. The sip from his bottle set fire to his throat, all the way down to his belly. Cobb had a habit of setting up a small distillery and brewing his own brand of alcohol. The men joked that if it ever leaked onto the rails, it would dissolve the steel into a worthless puddle. Bolt had often scoffed that that was an exaggeration, until he swallowed a mouthful of the stuff. Now he had to wonder why the ex-scout's eyes were only weak. Many a man had gone blind drinking home-brewed lightning.

Bolt had barely been conscious when they reached Proctor's personal car. He was aware of being stripped down to his drawers and having a strange man begin to treat his wounds. Cobb had been present and he and the surgeon bantered back and forth for a few minutes. After that, Ariette and the doctor were the only two in the room.

Finally, a damp cloth with a sickly sweet aroma was placed over his nose and mouth. He heard Ariette say: 'Go to sleep, darling,' and Bolt complied at once. He let go of his consciousness and slipped into a dreamworld, free of pain or thought.

Ariette awoke and wondered how long she had been asleep. Everything from the past couple days was a blur. She recalled staying at Bolt's side until he was sleeping restfully. The surgeon said he would return in a few hours and check on the patient. Meanwhile, Proctor's steward had drawn her a bath and prepared a bed for her. There had also been a pitcher of water and a plate of fruit and freshly made bread on a nightstand.

She didn't remember donning the long sleeping-shirt that had been laid out for her. She sat up, stretched her aching muscles and eased herself off the comfortable bed. She immediately curled her toes and walked on the sides of her feet to avoid the worst of her blisters. It would be some time before she could walk normally again.

She winced as she crossed the room on gimpy feet and looked into the wall mirror. It was next to a wash basin, beside which were a tall container of water, a hairbrush, a washing-cloth and soap.

Ariette groaned at seeing her reflection. Her eyes were red, with dark circles underneath. She had a scratch or two and a bruise she didn't even remember getting. Perhaps it was from flying chips of rock, or it could have been while battling through the underbrush, or while floundering about on the rocks like a dry-docked fish. As for the hair, it was tangles and knots from one side to the other. She had always been proud of her long, thread-fine hair, but, at the moment, she only saw it as a major chore to comb out.

Amazingly, the steward had washed and pressed her riding outfit. He – or someone aboard the train – had even patched a hole and mended several split seams or tears. Ariette worked for twenty minutes to make herself presentable, then she entered the main room of the luxury car.

'Ah,' Sirus Proctor greeted her, rising to a standing position from a leather-bound easy-chair. 'You look refreshed and completely recovered from your perilous adventure.'

Ariette sat down on a fancy divan to take the weight off her feet. 'You've been a most gracious host, considering you and Mr Mackintosh are rivals, competing for the same contracts.'

Proctor was not particularly handsome: a couple inches taller than most men but skeletal in build, with the thin features of a man who never found time to enjoy either food or life. He struck her as driven, but not to the point of criminal behavior. As to her observation, his smile never wavered.

'Win some . . . lose some,' he said easily. 'It's all part of the game. This is not the first time Mackintosh and I have gone head-to-head for a contract. I won the last time and he is going to win this one. It all evens out in the end.'

'I begin to see why Bolt did not think you were behind the kidnapping.'

Proctor laughed. 'Dear girl! I am a businessman, not a thug.'

'Yes, I can see that.'

'Would you care for something to eat? We ate lunch an hour or so ago, but the steward can round up 'most anything you like.'

'No, I sampled some of the fruit that was on the nightstand, before I went to bed. I was surprised that my outfit had been cleaned, darned and pressed.'

'My steward is wonderfully efficient,' Proctor said. 'Picked him up outside a pub in New York City. Poor fellow had just arrived from England and was robbed of every penny. He had been a servant on a large estate for a Lord somebody. Seems he had to pay a debt or something. Anyway, he was looking for a new life and I hired him on.

'That was fortunate for you both.'

'Fortunate,' he repeated. 'That's a word for Tug Mackintosh. He's the one who hired your friend, Bolterfeld – who's recovering nicely in the next room, I might add.'

'Then he is out of danger?'

'Unless he gets an infection he should be good as new in a few days. He's a very competent man. Wish I could steal him from Mackintosh.' He winked at her. 'Of course, you must know how well he can handle just about any job he undertakes.' With a sigh, 'I'd trade five of my best men for Mr Bolterfeld.'

'He seems devoted to Mr Mackintosh.'

The door opened and a new man – late twenties to early thirties – entered the room. He didn't remove his hat and stopped in his tracks when he spied Ariette. Slender, with similar features to Sirus, the man stared at her with a startled expression.

'My son,' Sirus introduced, 'Ripley. He's my all-around general foreman.'

Ariette inclined her head his direction at the introduction. Then her breath lodged in her throat and her jaw dropped. Her eyes widened in fright as she threw a quick look at Sirus.

'How did this woman get here?' Ripley demanded to know.

Sirus frowned at his son's harsh delivery. His gaze went from Rip to the girl and he grew more confused.

'My dear, what is it?' he asked, wondering about her alarmed look.

'Uh . . . nothing,' she said, masking her surprise. 'I . . . I just thought. . . .'

'Thought what?' Ripley snarled the words. 'Spit it out, woman!'

'Rip!' his father exclaimed. 'What has gotten into you?'

But his son continued to glare at Ariette. 'You recognized my voice, didn't you?'

Trapped in the dire situation, she replied: 'Actually, it was your boots. I've never seen a pair with those tiny medallions on the toes before.'

Ripley pulled his gun and pointed it at her.

'Son!' Sirus cried. 'What's gotten into you?'

Rather than answer his question, Rip threw a wild look of desperation at his father. 'How'd she get here?'

'Cobb brought her and Bolterfeld here late last night. Mack's foreman was shot up pretty bad and we were closer than his camp.'

'Damn it all!' Ripley lamented. 'That Bolterfeld completely derailed everything I had in place.'

'Talk sense, son.'

'He's trying to tell you that he's behind the murders and my kidnapping, Mr Proctor,' Ariette interjected. 'He hired those killers.'

Ripley cocked the trigger on his gun; Ariette gasped and threw up her hands to cover her mouth.

'Hold on!' Sirus bellowed. 'Is she telling the truth? Did you hire those men to kidnap this girl?'

'I did it to win the race and save us going deeply into debt.' Ripley snarled his reply. 'You and your ethics! You can't spend ethics, Father.'

'But we're not murderers and kidnappers.'

'It was a means to an end, and it would have worked . . . if not for Bolterfeld.'

'What is the gun for?' Sirus asked. 'What are your intentions?'

Ripley stared at his father. 'Time for you to make a choice, Father: me or them?'

The elder Proctor shook his head, confusion flooding his features. 'I don't understand.'

'There's a way out of this mess,' Ripley said, his mind working as he talked. 'I can't get us to Breakneck Pass first, but I can still walk away from this a free man.'

'I don't see how.'

'Wily came to see me yesterday. He said Bolterfeld and the girl had a good chance of escaping. He thought I ought to know.' Ripley laughed. 'As if I could ride away from my inheritance. I left the sap lying in a ditch.'

'Good Lord!' Sirus cried. 'What have I raised for a son?'

'It's your choice now, Father,' Ripley repeated the warning. 'If you go along with my story we can keep right on laying track and no one will ever know of my involvement. We finish up this job and move on to the next.'

'And if I don't like your story?'

Ripley narrowed his cold gaze. 'Don't make me choose between you and my freedom.'

'But what about the young lady here ... and Bolterfeld?'

'Wily is going to kill them both. Then I'll hunt him down for his treachery and bring in his dead body. No one will ever know I hired the Voights and the others.'

Sirus was stunned to the point of shock. 'You expect me to stand here while you kill this innocent girl and the wounded man in the next room?'

'You can turn your head or find the steward and make sure he doesn't see what is happening. Hate to have to shoot him too.'

'Son! I can't believe you could simply kill these people.'

'I been doing sabotage to slow our competitors for years. I just never told you, because you thought I was good for nothing but running errands like some gofer. I'm not going to run and hide without collecting what is due me.' Ripley showed an ugly sneer. 'Make up your mind, Father. Time is running out.'

Sirus lifted his hands in a helpless gesture, grief and dismay contorting his features. 'Please, son,' he begged, 'we can find a way to handle this. There must be a way to—'

'I knew you didn't have the guts,' Ripley jeered, shutting him up. 'I'll deal with it my way. If you can't handle it, that's too damn bad!'

At that moment the door swung open. Deek had his shotgun pointed at Ripley, ready for use.

'Drop the pistol, you dirt-wad kidnapper!' he hissed between his clenched teeth. 'I heard you from the other side of the door. Toss that iron or die where you stand.'

Ripley was in a bad position. His back was to Deek, his gun pointed in his father's direction. With

Deek's fingers on the twin triggers, he knew he had no chance.

There was a deadly quiet; no one dared take a breath. Then, unwilling to surrender his life, Ripley dropped his gun to the floor.

'Good thinking, son,' Sirus said in a dry, monotone voice. 'Smart of you to send the guard away so you could do your killing, except you got caught with your drawers around your ankles.'

Deek waited while Sirus called in the steward. His servant bound Ripley's hands and checked him for other weapons. He then summoned one of the foremen and Ripley was taken away to be locked up.

'He will stand trial at Cheyenne,' Sirus announced. 'However, I'll be getting him the best attorney money can buy.'

'Glad I didn't have to shoot him,' Deek said. 'My ribs are so tender from being shot . . . the recoil might have killed me.'

'How did you happen to arrive when you did?'

'Cobb came to town to deal with all of the bodies. He told me about Bolt and Miss Ekhard. I wasn't about to lie in a bed and wonder about the condition of the man who saved my life.'

'It would seem you saved both his life and mine too.' Ariette praised his timing. 'I'd say your debt has been paid twice over.'

'Well, Cobb told me something else that I could not wait to pass on.' He displayed a wolfish grin. 'You see, Big Mack has decided to marry Mrs Peterson, the woman who has been cooking and cleaning for him the past couple of years. That means you have been released from your promised marriage.'

Ariette sprang to her feet. She immediately grimaced from the pain, but remained standing. 'You mean it? My life is my own?'

'Far as Mackintosh is concerned, you're free to do whatever you want.'

With a happy chortle, Ariette started off towards the room where Bolt was. 'Oh, Romeo, Romeo,' she announced happily. 'I know where thou art, my Romeo.'

As she disappeared into Bolt's room Sirus frowned at Deek. 'What's with the Shakespeare?'

Deek shook his head. 'Got me. Must be a private joke between them.'

'Good of Mack to let her off the hook.'

Deek grinned, 'I reckon, in her and Bolt's case, a man could truly say: "*All's well that ends well!*"'

159